LOOSE THE DOGS

LOOSE THE DOGS

P.D. WORKMAN

ISBN: 9781988390260 (IS Hardcover)

ISBN: 9781988390253 (IS Paperback)

ISBN: 9781988390215 (KDP Paperback)

ISBN: 9781988390222 (Kindle)

ISBN: 9781988390239 (ePub)

ALSO BY P.D. WORKMAN

Zachary Goldman Mysteries

She Wore Mourning

His Hands Were Quiet

She Was Dying Anyway

He Was Walking Alone

They Thought He was Safe

He Was Not There

Her Work Was Everything

She Told a Lie

He Never Forgot

She Was At Risk

Kenzie Kirsch Medical Thrillers

Unlawful Harvest

Doctored Death (Coming soon)

Dosed to Death (Coming soon)

Gentle Angel (Coming soon)

Parks Pat Mysteries

Out with the Sunset

Long Climb to the Top (Coming Soon)

Dark Water Under the Bridge (Coming Soon)

Immersed in the View (Coming Soon)

Skimming Over the Lake (Coming Soon)

Hazard of the Hills (Coming Soon)

Reg Rawlins, Psychic Detective

What the Cat Knew

A Psychic with Catitude

A Catastrophic Theft

Night of Nine Tails

Telepathy of Gardens

Delusions of the Past

Fairy Blade Unmade

Web of Nightmares

A Whisker's Breadth

Skunk Man Swamp

Magic Ain't A Game

Without Foresight

Careful of Thy Wishes (Coming Soon)

Time to Your Elf (Coming Soon)

Undiscovered Tomb (Coming Soon)

Stand Alone Suspense Novels

Looking Over Your Shoulder

Lion Within

Pursued by the Past

In the Tick of Time

Loose the Dogs

AND MORE AT PDWORKMAN.COM

*Those who go beyond the call
to serve and protect*

PROLOGUE

"Of one thing I am sure," Glenn declared. "These dogs are perfectly harmless."

Burton studied him with a frown. It was a bold statement. And Glenn was the expert, the man they had made responsible to examine the psyches of these beasts. He was the one who was to help them decide the dogs' eventual fate.

"How sure are you?" he prodded.

"These dogs are not killers. They are house pets. Until recently, they were well cared for and had good relationships with their owners. I've talked to the family and neighbors. I've interacted with the dogs. You do not need to worry about it. They are good dogs."

"So your recommendation is to adopt them out."

"It would be criminal to put them down. What they did was purely for survival. It had nothing to do with aggression or violence. They are not going to hurt anyone."

"A lot of people are going to scream about them being killers if they are not put down."

"People will complain no matter what you decide. I already have a waiting list of people who want to adopt these dogs. One of them or even all of them together. I have more people than I can deal with."

Burton shook his head. "I don't think it is a good idea to adopt them out locally. Who knows what kind of weirdos we're going to get. Sure, there will be do-gooders who want to rehabilitate them or give them a good home. But how do you tell them apart from people who want a dangerous animal and will abuse them to increase aggression? Or people who want an animal with a reputation, something to show off. They'll get bored real fast, and you'll have the dogs back here to adopt out again. I don't know about dogs, but I know what happens to kids who keep getting shifted from one home to another."

Glenn nodded. "Same thing," he admitted. "Pretty soon they get identified as unadoptable, and we have to put them down."

"Rather unlike children," Burton clarified dryly.

"Right," Glenn chuckled. "That wouldn't be considered humane. Even though we would do it to our pets…"

"Different species, different laws. Okay. So we're going to have to do a press release. Announce they have all been examined by an expert, have been declared to be safe, blah blah blah, and will be adopted out. But we're not going to put them up locally, and we're not going to keep them together. We'll split them up and ship them all out to other cities."

Glenn shrugged. "If you have the connections to make those arrangements, great. And you're going to make sure the adopting families know the dogs' history…"

Burton shook his head, face flushing. His mouth tightened. "Not a chance. You've said they're safe. Knowing their history will have no impact on their behavior in their new homes. We're not going to tell people what happened. That will just cause the same problems as adopting them locally. Nice, quiet, stable families aren't going to adopt them. We need to get them into good homes. So they are well cared for, and there is no chance of any future violence."

Glenn swallowed. He looked at the floor, scuffing the tile with his foot. "Mr. Burton… I know you're the one making the decisions here, but I don't think that is wise."

"So you *aren't* one hundred percent sure the dogs are safe?"

"Yes, of course I am."

"Then why would we have to tell anybody what has happened here?"

"Just… because… they should know."

Burton shook his head. "No. No, no, no. That's the last thing they need to know."

CHAPTER ONE

Frank Horchuk would never forget walking into that trailer. He saw it in his mind every time he closed his eyes. He woke up in the middle of the night drenched in sweat, seeing those eyes and those teeth, screaming soundlessly, gasping for breath. Janice, his wife, had started sleeping in the other room, because even if Frank took sleeping pills, he still thrashed around in the throes of nightmares. He kept crying, wanting to hold her and to turn on the light. All of which, it would seem, upset her own sleep cycle.

The Johnsons' neighbors had reported something was wrong. They could hear the dogs howling and barking when they drove past. They hadn't seen Marion and Duane in many days, and Marion and Duane were always out and about; in the community visiting, fixing things, and of course taking the furry babies for walks. Everyone knew Marion and Duane. And they knew something was wrong. It had just been too long.

Frank had knocked and tried the door. There was no answer, and the door was locked. He tried to look through the windows, but it was summer, and the windows were blocked with tinfoil to try to keep the little trailer livable during the day. He could smell something putrid. He could hear the dogs, barking, and barking, but there were no footsteps, no one coming to the door. He took a walk around the trailer looking for anything suspicious. But there was nothing. Just the dogs barking wildly in the trailer. Barking at him to leave or to let them out. He wasn't a dog person. He wasn't sure what their particular tone of barks might tell a dog whisperer.

Frank tried again to look through the window, though he knew it was useless. He looked at the car, parked in the driveway. They only had one car registered to their names. The car hadn't been driven for several days. He could tell by the dust caked on it by the prairie wind. The muddy streaks from the morning dew. The car had been sitting there for a while. A good long while.

Eventually, Frank found himself on the doorstep again, this time taking out his lock aid to unlock the door. He fitted it in and pressed the button. Presto, the lock clicked. He turned the handle and paused before opening the door. He could hear the dogs moving frantically up and down the trailer. They weren't locked up or chained. And they weren't going to like an intruder.

"Hello?" he called. "Marion? Duane? This is Frank Horchuk, county police. Are you there? Do you need help?"

The dogs were on the other side of the door, barking, snarling, scratching at it. As he pushed it in ever-so-slowly, paws came around the door, grasping, trying to pull the door open far enough they could escape. He would have to step in with his leg blocking the door and push it shut behind him. Otherwise, the dogs would get out and be running loose on the property. Hoping they wouldn't bite him; hoping if they did, his heavy pants would protect his legs; Frank pushed his leg through the door, and slid the rest of himself into the trailer sideways, shutting the door behind him before those barking, snarling, furry babies of Marion's could escape.

Frank was immediately assaulted with the stench of the trailer. He could hardly breathe in the stifling enclosed space. He wanted to open the door immediately and slip back out. But he breathed through his mouth and waited for his eyes to focus in the dimness. There were no lights and the sunshine was well-blocked by the tin foil in the windows. He stood there, hands held out toward the dogs in a friendly, nonthreatening greeting. They were growling at him, but they didn't attack, and the barks had quieted. Some of them were whining.

As his eyes adjusted to the darkness, he closed them to shut out the gruesome sight. He couldn't physically bear to look at all of it at the same time. He held his hand over his eyes. He squinted through his fingers at one small part of the room, then closed his eyes again, breathing heavily through his mouth, and trying to process it before squinting again and immediately closing his eyes. He was like a child watching a scary movie on TV, pulled in by the fascination and curiosity, trying desperately to shut out the horror. It was too awful to take it all in.

The dogs had been shut in the trailer for a long time. The floor was caked with urine and feces. He might just have to retire his shoes after the call. But that wasn't the only smell. There was an overwhelming smell of decomposing flesh. The dogs had matted, dark muzzles. They'd been eating something and had not been properly cared for. Marion and Duane should have cleaned them up. Frank looked more carefully to see what they had eaten, though he had already seen too much. He already knew, his brain just couldn't accept what he had seen.

The desiccated remains of two bodies were laying in the living room. On the floor.

What was left of the bodies.

They were mangled almost too badly to be recognized as bodies anymore. Parts were missing, some of them scattered around the floor, where the dogs had each dragged their own portions to eat unmolested. Bits of bones and mangled flesh. Blood was spattered and smeared all over everything. The carpet, the walls, the dogs themselves.

The dogs were a sorry sight. Thin to the point of emaciation, their fur dull and matted. Their eyes crazy with fear. When he looked at the ones growling, they cowered before him, showing submissive behavior, even though he had made no threatening moves toward them. He reached slowly toward a golden retriever a foot or two away from him, rolling its eyes and crouching in submissive body language. As soon as he reached toward it, the dog's demeanor changed. It growled, showing its long sharp teeth. When he got too close, it snapped at him, and Frank jerked back, startled. He took a deep breath and tried to calm his heart.

Something was wrong. Something was very wrong.

A big black rottie advanced toward him, snarling. Long, pointed teeth, flecked with foam and blood.

Unable to comprehend what had happened, Frank turned the handle on the door behind him, slowly opened it and slipped back out. Slamming the door to the trailer, he stood on the front step, gulping down the cool, clean air, trying to clear his head and figure out what to do next.

It had been a long time before he was able to reach for his phone and call for backup and animal control. He stuttered and stammered on the phone, unable to describe what he had seen.

Those beasts, those horrible beasts. Were they the victims here? Abandoned to their own devices?

Or had they attacked their owners, unprovoked?

———

Frank was trying to focus on his model trains when Janice called him into the living room where she was watching the news. He knew by her voice something was wrong.

He hurried out, expecting to see a train wreck or a terrorist attack, maybe a hurricane off the coast of Florida where their daughter Elsie had just moved. Instead, he saw only a man in a suit, labeled 'Jim Burton' on the news screen, addressing a small scrum of reporters.

"What—" he started.

Janice waved him to silence. Frank stood back and listened to the suited man as he smiled and reassured the reporters.

"All of the dogs have been examined and watched by experts," he soothed, "and have been determined to be perfectly safe and nonviolent pets. They have been determined to be appropriate for adoption."

"The dogs…?" Frank repeated hollowly.

He saw them in front of him… the wet, matted muzzles. The crazy shine in the Rottweiler's eye as it advanced on him in the trailer, stifling with the smell of feces and urine and blood and decomposing flesh.

He heard all the dogs barking, snarling, and whining, as if they were so deranged they didn't even know what they felt.

And those bodies… torn to pieces… dragged around the room… pieces of bone and flesh hidden in corners, where each dog had dragged his own take.

The dogs were like ghosts. Like zombies, their ribs sticking out, their fur matted with blood, their eyes wild and crazy. They had tasted human flesh and Frank wasn't going to stick around to see how they liked it.

The reporters were all shouting questions at Burton, who was smiling serenely and nodding.

"They are not violent. They are not dangerous," he repeated. "We have had them examined by the top psychologist in the field. These dogs are the victims. They went through a terrible ordeal, and in the end, they did what they had to in order to survive. They didn't choose for this to happen. They didn't attack their owners. They were left to fend for themselves when their owners passed away of natural causes. They simply did what they had to in order to survive, the same as humans have been forced to throughout history. If we, being logical, thinking, moral creatures, can, in the direst of circumstances, be driven to eat human flesh, then why not these animals? They may love their owners, but after the weeks pass… they just did what they had to to survive. They are not a danger to their new owners."

"Who do our viewers talk to if they want to adopt them?" a pressed, coiffed woman at the front of the scrum asked.

There was shocked silence for a moment while the other reporters stared at her. Then they all looked to Horchuk for his answer.

"If you want to adopt a dog, you can go to the Humane Society and fill out a form," Burton said smoothly. "There is no special process for these dogs. There are no special requests for these dogs. They will go to the family they are best suited to, just like any other adoptable animals."

"But surely you will tell people if the dogs they adopt are part of this group?" one of the male reporters demanded.

"That's all the questions I can take right now. There are press releases on the table to your right. There are some binders of pictures of animals currently at the Humane Society for adoption. Thank you."

He walked away from the microphone, answering no more questions.

Frank stared in horror. "They are letting them go?" he said to Janice, in shock. "They are letting them all go?" He was aware he was shouting at her, even though it wasn't her fault. "Those animals should be destroyed! They are killers! You can't just unleash killers on an unsuspecting public!"

Janice shook her head, the expression in her eyes mirroring the horror and anger welling up in him. Outside the house, a dog barked. Frank jumped, his head whipping around to locate it. Again, he saw all those dark, wet muzzles surrounding him, barking, showing their teeth. Hungry, mad beasts.

He covered his eyes and rubbed his forehead, trying to wipe the images away. He dropped his voice. "Oh, Janice… how could they do this? How could they be so stupid?"

"Maybe they're right," she offered. "Maybe it was just a matter of necessity. We don't *know*."

"You didn't see those dogs," he snapped. "He—" Frank pointed at the TV screen, even though Burton was gone and forgotten by the cheerful news anchors back at the studio. "He never saw those dogs. How could anyone make such a stupid decision, knowing what they did?"

"We don't know they did anything wrong, Frank. They said the dogs didn't kill the Johnsons, they just… were starving, because no one was taking care of them anymore. It was just survival."

"How could they know? How can anyone know?" He was yelling, hurting his throat with the vehemence of his words.

"The autopsy—"

"Janice, all that was left was bones! How could they decide from the bones? I never even heard what the Cause of Death was. Did you hear a determination of Cause of Death?"

"I'm sure they must have figured something out." Her voice was calm, trying to make him see reason. "They wouldn't just release the dogs without knowing for sure, would they?"

"Wouldn't they? Bureaucrats! They just don't want to upset the bleeding hearts! The animal lovers! Well, you can love a wolf without unleashing it on the public!"

"But maybe they're right. Maybe they really are sure the dogs are not a danger."

"How can they be *sure*? They can't talk to the dogs. Even talking to a serial killer, people can't tell. The experts can't even prove what is going on in a person's head. How can they prove what is going on in a dog's head? If there is even a mental process. What if they just act on instinct? How can they be sure the dogs won't attack a live person? Is it really worth the risk?"

"I don't know… maybe they know," Janice repeated, stuck on that thought, unable to conceive that Frank could be right and the dogs could be killers.

"They don't know. If you put the dogs down, *then* you know. Then you know they'll never attack anyone again. If you let them go… if you let families adopt them—" Frank's brain flooded with pictures of babies and children, torn to bloody shreds.

"Oh no…" he moaned, holding his head. "If they let families adopt them… how can they risk children's lives like that?"

CHAPTER TWO

As they got ready to leave the house, Brenda swung the baby seat at her side. Her arm ached with the weight and she really hoped Erin would stop fussing and go back to sleep.

"I'm so excited," she said earnestly to Darren. She laughed. "Is it weird I'm so excited about getting a dog?"

Brenda was aware she was still often mistaken for a teenager. She'd managed to lose most of her pregnancy weight, and she was short and small-boned to start with. With her long brown hair pulled back into a ponytail and an easy smile, she looked like a high school cheerleader. Darren smiled indulgently.

"You've wanted a dog since before we got married. We are finally in a house of our own, where we can have pets. Of course you're excited."

"The kids are going to be so blown away," she giggled.

"Cassy won't know what to do with herself," he agreed. "She's wanted a dog ever since she could talk."

"We'll have to get one good with kids; a good family dog."

"I'm sure there will be a lot of them at the SPCA. We'll have our pick."

"Do you think it's right to go to the SPCA?" Brenda asked. "We shouldn't get a puppy, raise it all the way ourselves?"

Darren shrugged. "It's up to you. You said you didn't want to have babies in diapers and be house training a dog at the same time," he reminded her.

Brenda nodded, sighing. "I love puppies… they are so cute. But they are a lot of work. Peeing and teething, eating things and throwing up…"

"Just like kids," Darren teased.

"Yeah, just like kids. I don't want another kid right now. I want a dog. An adult dog."

"There's your answer, then. Don't worry about a puppy. It will be better to get a dog we don't have to worry will be nipping at the kids; something calm and sedate and used to children."

The baby started crying in earnest and Brenda sighed. She put the baby seat down and pulled the blankets back.

"You didn't sleep for long enough, silly baby. Why are you awake again already?"

Erin quieted a little but still kept whining. Brenda untucked the blankets and unlocked the buckle to remove the harness. She picked up the baby and jiggled her, kissing her blond curls.

"See, Erin? It's okay. What's wrong, are you wet?" She checked the baby's diaper and shook her head. "Hungry, then?"

Darren watched her, waiting for her to finish and re-engage with the conversation. Brenda dug a bottle out of the diaper bag and put the nipple in Erin's mouth. Erin took it hungrily. Brenda shook her head.

"You're not supposed to be hungry again already. I just fed you!"

"Maybe she had a bubble," Darren suggested. "She wasn't really full."

"I suppose. Well, I'll be a few more minutes, and then we can go."

"Okay. I'll put the stuff in the car."

He left Brenda with the baby and took the crate and treats out to the car. Brenda watched Erin feed, her eyes soft and loving. She glanced around the room.

"Pretty soon we're going to have a dog around here," she murmured. "Oooh, you're going to love growing up with a dog. You're just going to love having a dog. They can be such good friends."

She remembered the dogs she had while growing up. Especially Stanwick. He had been her best friend, her constant companion. He put up with anything she did to him and just loved her no matter what. She remembered sitting with him by the fire, taking him for walks, warming her feet underneath him as he slept on the bed. She supposed her memories were idyllic, tinted with rose-colored glasses. But it couldn't all be fantasy. She wanted her kids to have that experience, or some version of it. There would never be another Stanwick, but there would be something else… a Bowser, or a Rover, or a Spot. Every kid had to have a dog. Everyone should be able to feel that unconditional love.

Erin made gurgling noises, spitting out the nipple of the bottle. She gave Brenda a huge three-toothed smile, babbling nonsense. Brenda kissed Erin's round, pink cheek, a serene smile spreading across her own face. Then she bundled the baby back up again, strapped her into the baby seat, and headed out to the car to join Darren to go get the dog.

———

Darren came around the car as Brenda got out the baby seat, and took it from her.

"You're the one who is going to need your hands free," he commented. "So you can look around, and fill out the paperwork and all. I'll just be your slave today."

"And a very handsome one you are," Brenda teased good-naturedly, happy to have him take the weight of the baby carrier. Darren was not naturally drawn to help her out with the childcare or the housework. And despite his rugged look, he disliked working outside, preferring instead to let Brenda or hired students take care of the yard, while he cocooned with his computers and his music. He gave Brenda a half-smile, softening his often-tense expression. They went into the animal shelter, and after explaining to the receptionist they wanted to look around at the dogs before deciding what it was they wanted, they were shown which rooms the adoptable dogs were in and left temporarily to their own devices.

Brenda was in heaven roaming between the narrow aisles of cages, looking at all the beautiful dogs waiting for new homes. She wanted to take them all. It was so sad they had to be locked up there, waiting. And some of them… some of them would end up being destroyed. Darren, trailing along behind her, rolled his eyes when she would look back at him, cooing at this dog or that.

"It would be a lot easier to do this if it wasn't for the smell and the noise," he complained.

"Sorry," Brenda apologized. "Do you want to sit in the car while I do this? I guess I should have known it would bother you."

He shook his head, determined just to plow through. Brenda looked at him, frowning. Noise and obnoxious smells were not Darren's forte. He was the dad who would throw up over a dirty diaper. And the baby crying in the night or the other kids whining and getting rambunctious… it drove him up the wall. Brenda never quite understood how such normal, everyday life could bother him so much, but she accepted the fact that, like fingernails on a blackboard, some things were just more bothersome for some people.

"I'm going to be a while, Darren," she warned. "This isn't going to be quick."

He looked around. "We've been to almost all the rooms," he pointed out. "Then you can pick one out."

Brenda shook her head. "This is just the initial tour, to narrow it down. I'm going to have to watch the ones I like for a while, find out their histories, and hold them or play with them or walk them for a while, so I can see what they are like. You can't just pick one because it's cute."

"Oh… I thought that's what you were doing," he said, frowning.

"I like the cute ones," Brenda admitted. "That is part of it. But not the whole thing. You wouldn't buy a car without driving it, would you? No matter how sexy it looked."

"No way," he agreed immediately. "That would be stupid." He thought about it. "So you have to kick some tires. Take them out for a test drive."

Brenda nodded, smiling. "Yeah, you got it. But I'm not going to kick them."

"No, of course not." He didn't crack a smile at her joke. "So how long are you going to be. Should I take Erin home and come back later?"

"No, no. I won't be *that* long. And I might want to see how the one I pick interacts with you and Erin before I make a final decision. But it will be a while. You might want to go for a walk, or sit in the car. Go for gas or a car wash if you don't want to just sit."

Darren nodded. "Okay. I can do that," he agreed.

He retreated with the baby carrier, working their route in reverse, past the noisy, stinking dogs, eventually making it back to the reception desk.

"She's going to be a while," he explained.

The receptionist nodded. "Of course. These things take time."

———

Brenda continued to look at the dogs, wandering back and forth, reading the descriptive tags on their doors. She paid close attention to which ones were barking or wild and which ones were quieter and more sedate. She didn't want a dog that was going to bark all night and upset Darren. Or wake the kids. It would have to be a quiet, well-behaved dog. She gradually narrowed her short list down. One of the shelter workers approached her.

"Well, how's it going?" he asked.

"Good. I've got it down to three or four," Brenda gestured at one of the dogs she had passed a couple of times.

"Excellent. Why don't you come with me and we'll sit down and discuss your needs? Then we can talk about the specific dogs you've been looking at. How does that sound?

Brenda nodded. "Sure."

He led her back to a desk, crowded with papers and files. "Please, have a seat," he gestured. "I'm Bill."

"Brenda."

Brenda sat down while he dug out a form and started with the routine questions and whether she'd had a dog before. Brenda smiled, sitting back and telling him all about Stanwick. What a beautiful, loving dog he had been. Every child's dream best friend.

"And you're married now, with a baby," the man said, having noted Darren's and Erin's presence earlier.

"Yes. I have two other children as well; I didn't bring them along. They're at their grandma's. Cassy's two, and Bubba's four."

"Fun ages. We'll have to be really careful about the dog we introduce into the family. Kids can be unpredictable and we want a dog who can manage the situation."

"Right," Brenda agreed.

He ran through the costs to adopt and how much they would need to maintain a dog over the years. Since they didn't have any other pets, he gave her a list of vets in her area. Finally, he folded his hands on the desk and looked Brenda in the eye. He was an older man, a bit overweight, with a receding hairline and a fan of wrinkles around his twinkling blue eyes.

"Well. Shall we go find your dog?"

Brenda nodded eagerly, jumping to her feet. She laughed at herself. "I'm so excited about getting a dog. I feel like a kid getting up on Christmas morning."

He chuckled good-naturedly.

Brenda led Bill to the first dog she was interested in. It was a little Yorkshire terrier. He looked up at her, head cocked to the side, waiting for her to pick him out and take him home. Bill poked his fingers through the bars to give the little fellow a scratch behind the ears.

"How are you doing, boy? Hey? How are you?" He looked at Brenda. "Not a breed I'd recommend for children," he cautioned. "They are small, fragile, and tend to get nippy around kids. They're really not family dogs."

Brenda nodded. "Okay. Well, I don't want one that could bite the kids. So…"

She led him to the next one. A bigger dog, lean and dark brown, who looked up at them hopefully, eyes rolling back a little, showing the whites.

"Ah, now he's a nice choice," Bill approved. "We figure he's mostly Labrador retriever. Maybe some other breeds in the mix, but we think that's the main one. Retrievers tend to be good family dogs."

"I like his look," Brenda said. "Could I handle him?"

"Sure," Bill agreed. He unlatched the cage door and let Brenda enter.

Brenda held out her hand to the dog by way of introduction. He backed away from her, lowering himself closer to the ground.

"Hey, it's okay," Brenda soothed. "I'm not going to hurt you. How are you, buddy? How's my pretty dog?"

She approached again, and the dog rolled over on his side, raising his paws for her to scratch her belly, which Brenda promptly did.

"You're just a suck, aren't you?" she wheedled. "You're just a little wuss, looking for attention, aren't you? What a nice dog."

He whined a little, wriggling beneath her comforting touch. Brenda scratched his belly for a few minutes, then put her hand toward his head again. The dog put his head down and allowed her to scratch his ears and stroke his head.

"I think this is the one," she told Bill. "He's so gentle. He'll be a great dog for the kids. So friendly."

Bill nodded. "Okay. Why don't you take him out for a walk, introduce him to your husband, make sure they'll get along all right?"

Brenda nodded, smiling. She pushed a stray strand of hair back over her ear. She stood up, and the dog jumped back to his feet, yelping a bit.

"Oh, did I scare you? Silly boy!" Brenda scratched his head.

Bill pulled a collar and leash off of a nail on the wall and clicked his tongue at the dog.

"Come here, boy. Walkies."

The dog obediently went to him and was leashed. Bill handed the leash to Brenda.

"There you go. See how you get along."

"Heel," Brenda ordered. The dog shied away. "Come," she said in a lower voice, giving the leash a little tug. The dog followed, and once she got going, heeled nicely. She led him out of the building to get a little fresh air and see how they got along outside. She had taken him up and down the road a couple of times when Darren pulled up in a freshly-washed car.

"Did you choose one?" he asked when he got out of the car.

"Test drive," Brenda explained.

He nodded.

"Come on over, and we'll introduce you."

Darren approached slowly. He was anxious; not a dog person.

"It's okay, just relax," Brenda encouraged. "Don't act afraid. You want to act confident and relaxed, so he knows you're in charge. You're one of the top dogs in the pack. It's okay; I've got him on a short leash. He can't hurt you."

Darren came up closer and held out his hand. The dog sniffed at the proffered hand and rubbed against it, acting friendly.

"He's nice," Darren said, sounding a little surprised.

"Yeah, he is." Brenda was using her baby voice. "Isn't he a nice boy?"

The dog wagged his tail, looking at the two of them. Darren scratched the dog's ears, relaxing.

"Should I get Erin?" he asked.

Brenda nodded. "Yes. We'll make sure he's going to be okay around kids," she agreed.

Darren retrieved the baby seat from the car and looked at Brenda. "What should I do?" he asked.

"Just put the carrier down on the sidewalk."

Darren did so. Brenda let the dog get a little bit closer, still keeping the leash short. The dog sniffed curiously at the car seat, looking interested, ears pointing forward. Brenda pulled the blankets back from Erin's face. The dog got closer, poking his nose into the car carrier, sniffing vigorously. Erin started waving her fists and babbling. Brenda watched the dog for any sign of aggression. The dog looked back up at Brenda questioningly. Brenda laughed.

"It's a baby, silly," she explained.

Darren looked at her with a frown.

"I was talking to the dog," Brenda said.

"I know."

"You think it's weird because he can't understand me?"

He considered. "I think it's weird he doesn't know what a baby is."

"Oh." Brenda was taken aback. "Yeah, I guess he just wasn't in a house with a baby before."

"Do you think that's okay?"

"As long as everything else seems okay. We'll ask Bill to double check his history, just to make sure we don't have anything to worry about."

"Okay," he agreed. After watching the dog investigate the baby for a few more moments, he picked up the baby seat. "Just to be safe," he said.

Brenda laughed at his nervousness. "You're going to have to act a lot more confident around the dog or he won't listen to anything you say. Come on, let's go back in."

"Are you ready?" Darren stalled. "Because I don't want to go back in there if it's going to be a lot longer."

"Yes, I just have to ask Bill a few more questions, and fill out the forms. Then we'll be out of here."

Darren nodded. "Fine. Sounds good."

———

They went back into the building, and after a few minutes managed to track down Bill, touring another visitor around. He smiled at Brenda and nodded his acknowledgment then spoke to the couple he was showing around.

"Why don't you look around a bit? I just have a bit of paperwork to do, and then I'll catch up with you."

They murmured consent, and Bill broke away from them to deal with Brenda and Darren.

"And you must be Darren," he greeted, holding out his hand.

"Yes. And you must be Bill," Darren returned, reaching out to shake after a few awkward moments. He shook briskly and let go.

"Introductions done. So, how was he for you?" Bill asked Brenda.

"Good. I think he's going to make a great addition to the family."

"Excellent. Let's just finish up the paperwork and you can take him home."

"Can you tell me his background?" Brenda asked as they sat down at Bill's chaotic desk again.

"Oh, sure. Let me just pull up his file."

Bill tapped a few entries into his computer and looked at the screen.

"He was an out-of-state transfer. Probably an SPCA with an over-crowding problem. They try to send them out rather than putting them down. He was previously with an older couple. Retired."

"And why did they give him up?"

"They died. There was no one else to take him."

"Oh, how sad." Brenda rubbed the dog's ears and kissed him on the top of the head. "Poor little guy. I'll bet you were so sad."

Bill nodded.

"So, no experience with kids?" Brenda asked tentatively.

"Well, not in a home with kids. But that doesn't mean he didn't deal with them. There were probably grandkids, neighborhood kids, that kind of thing. No notes there are any problems with socialization or anything that needed to be addressed in his training or placement. And retrievers are usually good family dogs. Good with kids."

Brenda nodded slowly. "Okay."

"You do have a thirty-day return period," Bill pointed out. "If you get him home and find out he is acting aggressively to your son, you just bring him right back here. We don't want to push him on you if he's not a good fit. We'll find you another dog if he isn't the right one."

Brenda sighed. "That's good." She looked at Darren. "So if there are any problems, we're not stuck with him. We can change our minds."

"Right. That's helpful."

"So shall we get you signed up?" Bill asked.

Brenda nodded and broke into a grin again. "Yeah, let's get it done," she agreed with a big smile. She bent over to rub the dog's head again. "Let's get it done and take this baby home."

———

Brenda got the dog settled in the kennel and put the food bowls in the kitchen. She put a dog bed on the couch so there was somewhere he could lie down comfortably without getting his fur all over the furniture. Everything looked good.

She looked at the clock, waiting for the kids to get home. She was so excited for them to get home. She felt like there should be banners hung up, saying 'welcome home doggie.' It felt like Christmas. She would wake up early Christmas morning before the kids were awake and lay there in excited anticipation, waiting for them to wake up so she could watch them. She loved to watch their surprise, their happy faces. For her, that was Christmas.

She looked at the clock again. Not a minute had passed. She wanted them to be home. Sighing, Brenda went to peek out the front window, just to make sure they weren't back yet. But there was no car pulling up out front.

"They'll be home soon," Darren told her, noticing her anxiety.

"I know… I know. I'm just waiting…"

———

Finally, Brenda heard the front door open. The kids ran in, calling to her to tell her about their fun day with Grandma. Brenda smiled at her mother at the door.

"Come in, stay for a few minutes," she invited.

Grandma Rose knew what was happening, so she nodded and waited there to watch. Brenda bent down to hug Cassy and Bubba.

"Hi, guys! Did you have a fun time?"

"Mama, we had so much fun. We played at the park and we made cookies—"

"Cool. That sounds fun. Did you have a good time too, Cassy?"

"Mama…" she wasn't as verbal as Bubba. Words came with difficulty. Brenda waited patiently for her to get something out. "We play park; we make cookies."

"Yes, that's what Bubba said, isn't it? That sounds like a fun time."

"I play play dough," Cassy added, looking at her brother to contradict her.

"She played play dough, I didn't," Bubba said, playing the superior older brother.

"Play dough is good. I have a surprise for you today."

"Surprise?" Cassy repeated.

"What's the surprise?" Bubba asked, looking around excitedly.

"Something really great," Brenda teased.

Bubba started to pace the room, looking for the surprise. Brenda heard the dog yip in his kennel. Bubba had been looking under the couch and he suddenly stood straight up, listening, alert. He looked at Brenda, meeting her eye.

"Mama?" he asked tentatively.

She nodded.

"No way!" Bubba shouted. He ran out of the room to the back door, where the kennel was located. "Cassy, come here!" he shouted.

Cassy pattered after him. Brenda and Grandma Rose followed them to the back door and watched as Bubba circled the cage, looking at the dog from all angles. Cassy, staring in amazement at the dog, crouched a few feet away.

"Mama, it's a dog!" Bubba exclaimed. "It's a dog for us?" he demanded.

"Yes, Bubba," she agreed.

"A dog for us!" Bubba yelled at his sister.

Cassy looked at him, her eyes sparkling.

"Doggie for us?" she echoed to him, and then she turned and looked at her mother. "Doggie for us?" she repeated.

"Yes, Cassy," Brenda assured her.

Bubba stuck his fingers in through the bars of the kennel. The dog yipped and turned frantic circles inside the cage.

"Brenda," Grandma Rose said warningly.

"No, Bubba," Brenda corrected. "Don't put your fingers in. You're making him upset. We've got to keep him calm, and then you'll be able to pat him and play with him. Okay? We have to give him a chance to get used to a new place and the new people."

Bubba pulled back his fingers. Brenda could see he really wanted to put them back in and touch the dog.

"You'll get to touch him, Bub. Just not right now. When an animal is in a cage, if you stick your fingers through the bars, you could get bit. Animals bite when you stick your fingers through the bars."

"Oooh," he said, and put his hands in his pockets.

"Mama," Cassy tugged on her arm. "Mama, mama!"

"What is it, Cassy?"

"Mama. Doggie name?"

"Oh." Brenda smiled down at the pudgy little girl. "The doggie doesn't have a name yet. We have to think of one."

"I know a name!" Bubba shouted.

"What, Bub?"

"Rover. You could call him Rover. Or Bumblebee."

Brenda looked at him, bemused. "Bumblebee?"

"Yeah!"

"We'll have to think about that. We have to find a name that fits him."

"Kitty," Cassy contributed sweetly.

"What?"

"Name Kitty."

"But he's a puppy, Cass."

Cassy nodded seriously. Brenda shook her head at her silly children. She could see she was going to have to be the one to name the dog. Darren wouldn't have any interest in it, and the children were going to pick something ridiculous. The dog deserved a proper name, like Stanwick. He'd always been happy with his name; and it was something dignified, good for a Great Dane, nice and solid. It wouldn't work for the new dog, of course. She needed something a little warmer and friendlier. And the dog was shy. She'd have to take all those things into account in picking out a name.

"Mama, when are you going to let him out?" Bubba asked.

"Not for a while. He needs to get used to you and Cassy being around, okay? You can go find something to do now and I'll call you for supper."

"Is he going to eat supper?"

"He'll eat his own supper. Dog food, not people food."

"He dog," Cassy contributed, directing this at Bubba.

"I know he's a dog," he said, rolling his eyes.

"Him eat doggie food."

"Cassy, go away!" Bubba snapped. "You're bugging me."

Cassy looked at him for a minute, then left the room. Brenda raised a brow at Bubba.

"You need to be more polite to your sister. You might have hurt her feelings."

"No, I didn't," Bubba assured her.

Brenda looked at him for a minute, then shrugged. "You go find something to do too. You'll get to pat the dog later, okay?"

He rolled his eyes theatrically, and with a big sigh, headed out of the room. He stopped in the doorway and turned back.

"Mama?"

"Bub?"

"I really like the new dog. Thank you for getting him."

Brenda smiled, her face getting warm. "Thank you, Bubba. I'm glad you like him. I think it's going to be great having a dog around here."

"Me too," he agreed.

Then he left the room. Brenda looked at Grandma Rose. "Well, what do you think?"

"We should have videotaped it. That was just so sweet. They're going to love having a dog."

"I know," Brenda agreed. "And me too. I've been waiting so long, living in all these places where we couldn't have a dog. I'm happy to finally be able to have one."

"And how do you think this little fella is going to do? He's not a puppy."

"I didn't want a puppy. I still have two kids in diapers! I think he's going to do great. He's gentle and shy. He won't be mean to the kids."

"Good. And he doesn't have a name yet? What are you going to call him?"

"I forgot to ask the Humane Society what his previous owners called him. I guess it doesn't matter; I'll train him to answer to something else. But it would have been good to know. Might help the transition."

"Are you going to let Cassy call him Kitty?" Grandma Rose asked mischievously.

Brenda laughed. "No, not a chance. You can't call a dog Kitty; it'll get an inferiority complex!"

"Cats think they are superior. Maybe it will give him a superiority complex."

Brenda giggled. She turned around to face the counter. "Do you want a coffee?" she asked.

"I would love one. Then I'd better leave you to supper."

Brenda put some coffee grounds in the machine and leaned against the counter while she waited for it to perc.

"So, how were the kids at your house?"

"Good, as always. Not much fighting today. Bubba is getting better with Cassy."

"And she's getting to be more and more like a little person. Bubba's getting rambunctious, I'll be glad when he's in kindergarten. He needs more to keep his attention. Somebody else watching him so I don't have to do it all day."

"Don't wish away your time. Enjoy it while he is still a preschooler and don't wish he was older all the time. You'll miss these days when they are all teenagers."

"I know. But he's at a sort of awkward, in-between age. I think he's ready for school."

"Good. Better for him to start when he's ready than too early. And if Cassy's in preschool half days, then you'll be able to spend some quality time with the baby. And the dog!"

"I'm looking forward to it. I think I might get back into running. It will be good for me, and the dog will keep me going out."

———

Brenda let the dog out of the kennel. She carefully put the leash on the dog, murmuring to him.

"There, that's a good boy," she approved. "You sit nice for me, don't you? Good boy."

The dog whined slightly and lay down on the floor, raising his paws for her to scratch his belly. Brenda smiled and rubbed his stomach.

"There you go, you wuss."

She waited for him to get back up, and then put her hand on his head.

"Good boy. Stay."

She waited until he seemed calm and settled, then called for the kids.

"Cassy, Bubba, you can come in and see the dog now."

The children ran across the house to the kitchen and cooed excitedly over the dog. Brenda patted him to keep him calm.

"Okay, come over here, and move slow. Show him the back of your hand. Let him smell you."

"Like this?" Bubba asked, holding out his hand toward the dog.

"Yup, that's right. Just sit there and let him smell you for a minute."

Bubba kept still, holding his hand there. The dog sniffed him for a few minutes, and then rubbed against Bubba's hand. Bubba grinned.

"He likes me!" he exclaimed.

"Yes, he does," Brenda agreed. "You're doing a good job."

"Me?" Cassy asked.

Brenda nodded. "Just like Bubba," she agreed, "show him your hand first."

"'Kay," Cassy agreed.

She squatted close to the dog and held out her hand, trying to move exactly as Bubba had. The dog sniffed at her, and eventually he rubbed against her hand too.

"Like him," Cassy cooed.

"Yes, you like him, and he likes you."

Brenda rubbed the dog's head. "You're a good dog. Aren't you doing so well to sit here quietly," Brenda said.

The dog rolled his eyes back. Brenda continued to rub his head affectionately.

Cassy left and came back with a bag of doggie treats in her hand.

"Him eat?" she asked.

Brenda laughed. "You're too smart for your own good, aren't you?" she accused.

She took the bag from Cassy. The dog sat up, very interested in the bag of treats. He sniffed and nosed at it and pawed at it with his front paw. He whined, a high-pitched whine.

"Be patient," Brenda remonstrated. "You'll get some."

She opened up the bag and pulled a biscuit out. She held it in her hand.

"Do you want a treat?" she asked.

The dog strained to get at it. He yelped. Brenda held it still, waiting.

"Sit," she ordered.

After a moment of straining for the treat, the dog did. He sat there, watching the treat, his body shivering with anticipation.

"Good dog. Lie down?"

The dog didn't move.

"Lie down," Brenda repeated more firmly this time, and she held the treat close to the ground. The dog moved toward it to snatch it away from her.

"No. Lie down," Brenda snapped, pulling the treat away. "Come on. Sit." The dog behaved. "Now lie down."

She pressed on his shoulder and reluctantly, he obeyed.

"Good boy. Now stay."

There was a noise in his throat halfway between a whine and a growl, sort of a grumble, and the dog kept his head down between his paws, watching her movements. Brenda waited, watching for any movement. Once satisfied, she held the treat out.

"Good boy. Here's your treat."

He snatched it from her hand so sharply it made Brenda jump.

"You are impatient, aren't you? Well, at least you stayed like you were supposed to. We'll have to work on that. Grabbing is rude, you know."

"Rude," Cassy echoed.

"That's right," Brenda said.

"He does good tricks," Bubba declared. "Doesn't he, Mama?"

"He does well. But he needs a bit of polish. I think he might have been spoiled a bit at his last home. We have to make sure he knows there are rules here. That will keep everybody happy."

"Daddy doesn't like him," Bubba said.

Brenda frowned. "What? Did Daddy say that?"

Bubba shook his head. He assumed a different posture. It was obvious he was imitating his father.

"That dog better stay off of the couch and not jump up on me," he said in a lofty voice.

Brenda rolled her eyes. "Well, like I said, we'll teach him to follow the rules, and then everybody will be happy. Including Daddy. Because the dog won't get fur all over the couch or jump on Daddy. Will he?" She directed this at the dog, who looked up at her while crunching his biscuit and had no answer for her.

"But you put his bed on the couch," Bubba pointed out. "So how can you make him stay off of it?"

"He can only sleep on his bed. That will keep fur from getting on the rest of the couch. It's okay if he sleeps on his part of the couch, just not on Daddy's!"

"Or mine," Cassy put in.

"Okay, or yours," Brenda agreed. "He'll stay off everyone's part of the couch, and he'll only sleep on his bed."

"Okay," Bubba said uncertainly. "I suppose so…"

Brenda shook her head at the attitude and mannerisms he picked up from his father even when he wasn't mimicking him. It was cute.

———

"How about Jake?"

Darren rolled over in bed, trying to pry his eyes open and focus in on Brenda.

"What?" he asked muzzily.

"For the dog's name. I like Jake."

Darren wiped his face with both hands. "Yeah. I like Jake just fine," he agreed.

"Is it too simple? Too common? I want a good name, but not something everyone else has used."

Darren cleared his throat. "No, you're right," he agreed.

"So you think it's too common of a name?"

"I think it's up to you. Do you think it's too common?"

He couldn't figure out why she was bringing this up in the middle of the night when he was half-asleep after a long day's work. Why would he care what she named the dog? As long as the dog knew its name and responded to it.

"Oh, you're no help," she snapped.

Darren analyzed her tone. Was she playful, or really irritated? Had he screwed up?

"Sorry," he said slowly.

"No, you're right. It's my choice. You don't even like the dog."

This time, he was pretty sure she was being sarcastic. Darren had no clue where this was coming from. He thought he had been very supportive of her desire to get a dog. He'd even gone to the pound with her.

"I like the dog fine," he said. "Did I tell you I didn't like it?"

"You apparently told the kids."

"The kids… no, I'm pretty sure I didn't."

"Bubba thought you did. So you do like him? You're not mad about me getting him?"

"No. I wanted you to be happy."

"Oh, good. Well, think about Jake, okay? Do you think it's a good name for him?"

Darren took a deep breath. He lay there staring at the ceiling, counting the seconds. He wanted her to think he was thinking deeply about this. It was somehow important to her. So he gave it due consideration before coming up with an answer.

"He looks like a Jake," he said. "I think that's a clever name. Do you think it suits him?"

"Yes, I really do. I look at him, and I think, 'that's Jake.'"

"Well then, it doesn't matter what anyone else thinks, does it? If that's the right name for him, who cares how many other Jakes there are out there?"

Brenda nodded excitedly. "You're so right! I know a lot of people didn't like 'Bubba,' but that didn't stop us from naming him Bubba. It was just the right name for him, and if anyone didn't like it, then too bad. It suits him."

"Right," Darren agreed. He had never admitted it to her, but he was one of those who didn't like the name Bubba. But over the years, it had grown on him, and now he couldn't imagine his son named anything else.

The name had grown on him, or Bubba had grown into it. Now, Darren was convinced it had been the right choice. And if she needed confirmation the dog's name was right, he was happy to supply her with that too.

"Bubba is Bubba," he said with finality. "And the dog is Jake. Let's celebrate in the morning."

Brenda made a little cheer and cuddled up under his chin, making a purring sound. "You're the best, Darren. You always know what to say."

He breathed a sigh of relief, tightened his arms around her to give her a squeeze, and closed his eyes to go back to sleep again.

CHAPTER THREE

"How are the new recruits?" Steven asked.

Shirley pushed her unruly gray hair back over her ear and looked over the kennels of dogs, though she had already assessed them herself. None of them were barking or standing up against the chain link. They were sitting or standing, watching her and Steven with interest. Not too hyper, not noisy or aggressive. But on the same note, none of them were just lying down sleeping, either. Ears pointing forward, they had a healthy interest in what the humans around them were doing. She was happy with the initial lot.

"Pretty good," she said, hands on hips. "The SPCA is doing a better job at prescreening them now. We don't get any that are obviously incompatible. Which is great, because our training program can be spent on training dogs with the aptitude for it instead of on initial prescreening."

"Excellent. Glad to hear it. Do we have complete histories on all of them?"

"No, not all of them. Some are strays with unknown pasts, or transfers from out of the city, and we don't have extensive histories for them. But we'll watch them carefully. We'll know if there are any problems. Are you going to stick around for some of the training?"

"I'd like to see them put through their paces," he agreed. "I won't stay for long, but I'd like to see the quality of dogs we're getting."

"Sure. Just stay to the side and don't try to interact with them."

He nodded. "Wouldn't dream of it."

———

Shirley motioned to her handlers.

"Okay, let's get the first round of dogs out," she instructed. "Then gather around for a minute."

They took the first half dozen dogs out of their kennels, attached leashes, and gathered around Shirley. She was happy to see none of the dogs tried to make a break for it before their leashes were on. While some of them were interested in exploring or in greeting the dogs next to them, none of them yanked on their leashes. They all stuck close to the side of their handlers on a short leash and didn't complain.

"Great. This looks like a good bunch," Shirley acknowledged. "First, let's test their knowledge of basic commands and their obedience. Verbal commands only; sit, stay, heel, and so on. Take them through their paces and see if there are any initial problems."

The handlers spread out across the compound to do as she had instructed. Shirley walked around, watching the dogs for any sign of problems. They didn't want dogs that were aggressive. They needed dogs that obeyed immediately and didn't have to be told more than once. It was important to have a good foundation to begin with.

She watched Christine handling a beautiful German shepherd. She was a new trainer, a twenty-something strawberry blond who seemed to possess the necessary intelligence and animal empathy for the job. The shepherd was an apt pupil, engaged and interested, obeying Christine's commands. Obviously not a show dog; when commanded to heel, he didn't walk as closely to her as a show dog would, and his pace was slightly uneven as he watched the other dogs around him. Not quite distracted, but definitely aware and interested.

"Down, " Christine told him firmly. "Stay."

The dog lay down as he was told, resting his chin in his paws. Christine watched him for a moment to see if he was going to bound up again the moment she broke eye contact. She dropped the leash, turned, and walked away from him. The dog raised his head, watching her walk away with bright interest. He didn't get to his feet or try to creep after her. He didn't whine or bark. But he didn't go to sleep, either. He watched her walk out of sight behind a fence and waited for her to return. Some time passed, and he continued to watch intently for her return. A couple of times, he turned his head to watch another dog who got close to him, but he turned back to watch for Christine's return.

After a few minutes, Christine appeared from behind the fence and walked back to him. He thumped his tail on the ground appreciatively, but he didn't get up or move toward her. Christine picked up the leash.

"Good boy," she praised. "Sit."

He sat back up, wagging his tail.

"Nice dog," Shirley approved.

Christine nodded. "Isn't he a sweetie? He seems pretty well-trained on the basics. Do you want me to try him on hand signals?"

"No, spend a bit more time on foundation. We'll keep everybody on the same schedule for now."

"Sure, no problem." She looked back at the dog. "Heel!"

She took off briskly across the compound, weaving around other dogs and pylons. The shepherd stuck close behind her.

———

"Okay," Shirley addressed the group of handlers. "For those of you with nameless dogs, I need you to choose a name soon. We want to get them used to them as soon as possible. We only want them to obey commands when they are given by their usual partner or by name. We don't want a perp to be able to tell them to lie down. It needs to be something short and clear. Something that can be whispered or yelled and be understood equally either way. And it needs to be an appropriate name. We don't want the perp to fall down laughing when he hears your dog's name!"

Shirley looked at Christine.

"What are you calling your dog?"

"I thought maybe 'Bandit,'" Christine suggested.

"Bandit catches the bandits, huh? Well, I suppose it's better than Killer. Get him used to it."

"I will."

"How's he been doing?"

"Good. Seems to be a good pupil. Obeys pretty well; seems eager to learn."

"Shepherds are good police dogs. They like to please you. They have lots of intelligence. Pick things up quickly."

Christine nodded.

When Christine took Bandit off of his leash, she broke the rules just a bit. She got down and cuddled him and scratched his ears, talking baby talk. She knew she was supposed to be the alpha dog and demand his respect, but she loved him and was impressed with his desire to please.

"You're a good boy, aren't you, Bandit?" she crooned.

She fed him a few treats she had kept secreted away in her pocket. "You've been such a good boy. You're such a good learner. Aren't you? I don't know why anyone would let you go to the pound. It's a crime." She giggled to herself. "Well, now you're the crime fighter, right?"

Someone walked into the hall, and she quickly stood up and put Bandit into his kennel.

"There you go, boy. I'll see you in the morning."

He went in and sat down, watching her latch the gate again. He whined in the back of his throat so softly she almost couldn't hear it.

"Night night. Have a good sleep. Tomorrow we'll go fight some crime."

CHAPTER FOUR

Brenda loved having a dog in the house. And Jake was the perfect family pet. He was never aggressive toward her or the kids. He was happiest just lying and watching her work. He was usually obedient, though sometimes he refused to lie down when she asked him to. And she had caught him a few times sleeping in Darren's spot on the couch instead of in his doggie bed. He went contritely to his bed when she told him off, but the look he gave her once he was lying down in his bed… she sometimes wondered just what he was thinking. It was almost as if he was trying to usurp Darren's place or to demonstrate to Brenda his disdain for his master.

Darren had little to do with the dog, but that was okay. They had understood when they started this whole thing he really was not a dog person. It would be her job to look after him and make sure Jake had everything he needed. She certainly never thought Darren was going to take Jake out for walks or pick up his poop.

Bubba was both grossed out and fascinated by Jake's feces, thinking it was the greatest joke in the world that they had to follow the dog around and pick up his poop. What could be more hilarious for a four-year-old boy? Cassy turned up her little pug nose and would have nothing to do with the picking up after such a disgusting animal. She only wanted to deal with Jake when they were inside. She loved to dress him in a bonnet and take pictures of him, his long-suffering eyes rolling up to the ceiling.

The kids were both off to preschool. Brenda quickly changed into her running clothes. It seemed like the half-day they were gone was shorter and shorter every day. When they had first started preschool, it had seemed like they were gone forever. She would be watching the clock, waiting for preschool to end and for them to be home. But she had grown used to her alone time, and there were so many things she put off for when she was alone and could do them without interruption. She was trying to get back into running, and like she'd told her mother, the dog was good incentive. Jake loved to go running with her.

He heard her getting the jogging stroller out and came into the room, watching her with thoughtful eyes.

"Yes, you're right, we're going out for a run, Jake," Brenda told him. "Do you want to go out for a run?"

He whined an answer.

"Good. You stay, and I'll get Erin and the leash."

He stayed put until she put the leash on him, then began dancing around happily, playing with the lead and being goofy. Brenda laughed.

"You're such a clown," she told him.

She got the jogger and the dog out the door and started off slowly. The day was brisk and clear. She started out with a slow warm-up pace. Jake was prancing beside her and pulling on the lead, wanting to go faster.

"Wait a bit, Jakey. I have to get warmed up first. You don't want me to injure myself and have to go home."

Jake looked at her reproachfully. Go home already?

"That's right; you don't want to, do you? So be a good boy and just run nice until I get up to speed."

She pushed the stroller along ahead of her, enjoying the fresh breeze. She soon left the city streets to get to one of the riverside pathways they enjoyed so much. She knew she was lucky to live in a town with such a beautiful pathway system. She could go for hours without having to run on a city street until it was time to go home again. Of course, she didn't have hours to run and hadn't yet built up her endurance to that level. But she could when she was in better shape and had the time.

After a few minutes, she was loosened up, and she picked up her pace a bit. Jake ran beside her, loving stretching his muscles, actually getting to run like a dog was meant to. His tongue hung out as he ran, and Brenda wondered if his tongue didn't get dry and gritty running with his mouth wide open. But if so, he didn't seem to mind.

———

After running for a while, Brenda slowed for a break. Erin was starting to sound cross, and they were at a park with a water fountain so she could stop and rehydrate. She let Jake off the leash.

"Off-leash area, Jake. But you have to stay close, or I'll get in trouble."

He huffed at her, excited to run free.

"Do you want a drink first?" Brenda suggested, moving to the fountain.

He turned and looked at her for a moment, then conceded to come over to the fountain. He stood on his hind legs, tail wagging slowly, and waited for Brenda to turn it on. Brenda obliged, and he lapped at the water mid-air. She wasn't sure how much he got, but it was better than nothing.

"Okay, go explore," she told him. "But only for five minutes, then we're going to run some more."

He stepped down, and Brenda had a drink while he went to investigate the various trees and shrubs in the small park. Brenda bent over the jogger to talk to Erin.

"And what are you fussing about? Here you get this nice free ride, get to watch the world go by with no effort of your own, and you're complaining?"

Erin whined and grumbled, and Brenda dug out some baby crackers and put them on her tray.

"Just a few, because you can't eat while I'm running. I can't see your face, and wouldn't know if you were choking."

Erin grabbed one of the crackers and started to gum it. Brenda stood up, pushing her hair back from her face. She looked around to see what Jake was up to. He was lying down in the grass and leaves, sneaking up on a squirrel foraging in the open area. Brenda chuckled about the big dog thinking he was a mighty hunter. Dogs were always too excited when they treed a squirrel. Never mind a three-year-old boy could do the same thing. When a dog did it, it was something special. She watched Jake, waiting for him to dash out into the opening and scare the squirrel up the tree. Jake crept closer and closer, hardly rustling the leaves. He was a much better hunter than Brenda would have guessed.

Then with a loud bark, he leaped into the air and landed on top of the squirrel. Brenda let out a shout.

"Jake, no!" she yelled. She ran toward him. "Don't kill it, Jake! No!"

She was far too late. She had underestimated his abilities, and she was too late. He had killed the squirrel on landing and was now savaging his prize, grimly pleased with himself. Brenda ran up to take it away from him. He snarled when she got close. Brenda realized taking his kill away from him was not a good idea right now. She knew better than that! But in all the years she had grown up with dogs, she had not seen them kill. All her dogs had been city dogs, with little hunting instinct. Comfortable inside the house, not out in the wild.

"Oh, Jake. Why did you do that?"

He was watching her, tearing at the squirrel, one eye on her at all times to make sure she couldn't take away his prize. Brenda didn't know what she was going to do. She couldn't leave the dead squirrel in the park, nor could she pick it up. At least not until he was finished with it.

"You're not hungry," she told him. "You didn't kill it so you could eat it."

He growled as he gnawed on it. Brenda wasn't sure whether he was actually eating, or just chewing on it for the fun of it. She eventually realized she had to go back to the stroller. Erin had finished her crackers and was squalling for attention. Brenda walked back to the abandoned stroller and talked to Erin, waiting for Jake to abandon his prize so she could clean up after him. She was no longer interested in continuing the run. She just wanted to get home and forget about this part of her day.

———

Darren noticed Brenda was unusually quiet and a bit short with the kids. She was usually pretty relaxed after they got home from preschool, and they had a nice evening having dinner and playing a bit before they went off to bed. But it seemed like she had a black cloud over her.

"Do you want me to put the kids down?" Darren asked as Brenda rinsed the dishes, squawking about them getting underfoot.

Brenda looked at him, her face tense and tired. "Are you sure?" she asked. "I can do it…"

"No, let me. You look like you could use a break."

Brenda nodded. "I really could. Thanks."

He called the kids to follow him and got them started on their bedtime routine. Daddy putting them to bed was novel, so they didn't dawdle or backtalk. They got ready and did the things he asked them to and acted like they were having a good time doing it.

Brenda sighed a long, slow hiss of air. She stared down at the dirty dishes; her shoulders slumped in fatigue. She didn't know what was wrong with her. She couldn't get the picture of Jake attacking the squirrel out of her mind. How lame was that? It was a good thing she wasn't a country girl. Imagine getting sick over the killing of a rodent. Anybody else would have just left it there, or tossed it in the garbage without another thought. They wouldn't have gagged or shed tears over it. One less vermin in the city. Who would cry over that?

It took a great effort to finish the dishes and start the machine running. Brenda plopped down on the couch in front of the TV, not even bothering to grab her basket of laundry to sort and fold. She just couldn't manage it. Her brain was too full of other things. Darren was out a little while later and sat down beside her. He put his arm around her, looking at her face.

"Is something wrong?" he asked. "You seem like you have something on your mind."

"No," Brenda said. Though of course there was. And of course, she wanted him to pursue it more strenuously. He studied her.

"Are you sure? You seem upset."

"I just had a hard day; that's all."

"Yeah? Why don't you tell me about it?"

Brenda shook her head. "Just stupid stuff. You know how sometimes things just don't fall into place like you want them to. That kind of day."

"Oh. Okay."

He picked up the remote and flipped through channels to see what was on. Brenda watched him, waiting for him to ask her more about it.

"Do you think getting Jake was a mistake?" she asked finally.

Darren looked at her, surprised. "A mistake? I thought you love that dog."

"I do. I just wonder… I mean, a dog is a lot of extra work, and what with the kids around and being so young…"

"They told you that you could take him back if it didn't work out," Darren ventured.

"I know. I don't want to give him back. I just wonder… maybe it wasn't the right time."

"If he's too much work…"

"No. I just think I might have jumped the gun a bit."

"Okay," he drew the word out as if doubting what she said.

Brenda turned her face away from him to watch the TV. He followed her example and turned back to the show he had landed on. He stared at the screen and didn't look back at Brenda to see the tear running down her cheek.

How stupid. She berated herself. What was she crying over? Over a squirrel? Over the fact the dog had the instinct to hunt rodents? She wasn't even crying over the fact Darren didn't dig deep enough to tease out what the trouble really was. It was just all overwhelming. Maybe she was still feeling a bit of postpartum blues. It should be gone by now, and running with the dog should help, but there was no reason she couldn't still be feeling a bit postpartum. A bit hormonal. Her ridiculous tears could be excused.

Brenda put her head on Darren's shoulder. He put his arm around her to hold her close, kissing the top of her head.

"Just have a rest," Darren murmured. "It will all look better in the morning."

———

Brenda felt bad the next day about overreacting over Jake killing the squirrel. He was just responding to instinct, after all. It wasn't his fault. As soon as they had gotten home, she had put Jake in his kennel and had left him there the rest of the day, other than to take him outside and to feed him. It wasn't his fault, and she shouldn't have treated him like he was a bad dog.

She let Jake out of his kennel in the morning and let him out to the back yard. When he was done his business, she fed him.

"You're a good dog, aren't you Jake?" she murmured.

He eyed her and growled lowly.

"Hey, what's that about? I'm not going to take your food," she protested.

He looked back down at his food and ignored her. Brenda let him eat in peace, deciding it was best not to push her luck.

————

She heard Bubba and Cassy squealing upstairs. One of them had obviously woken and gotten the other one up. She glanced at the clock. How long did she have before they were downstairs? Brenda got out the cereal and milk and put bowls on the table, setting them down just as the children ran down the stairs squealing at each other.

"Mama! Mama, Bubba…" Cassy was wailing.

"Oh, shush, come sit down and have some breakfast. No tattling this early in the morning."

"But Mama—"

"Shush, Cassy. Sit."

"I didn't do anything," Bubba objected.

"You too. Sit."

Bubba scampered across the floor toward Jake, who was still eating.

"Bubba, leave Jake—"

Before she could finish the warning, Jake whirled around with a snarl and snapped at Bubba. Shocked, Bubba froze and stared at Jake. Brenda ran across the kitchen and grabbed him, picking him up and spinning him away from the dog.

"Bubba! I told you not to get close to Jake while he's eating! Dogs don't like it when you get too close to their food. They think they have to guard it."

Bubba's face crinkled up, and he started to blubber.

"Mama! Mama, he tried to bite me!" he shrieked, between hysterical sobs.

"It's okay. He wouldn't really bite you. He was just warning you. You're okay."

Bubba cried, burying his face in her shoulder. Cassy, sitting at the table, started to cry in sympathy.

"Mama…"

"Shhh," Brenda comforted. "Come on guys; it's okay. You're both fine. Bubba's fine, Cassy. He didn't get hurt."

They both continued to cry. Brenda took Bubba into the living room, motioning for Cassy to follow her.

"Come on. Come sit down and calm down."

She cuddled them both on the couch until they started to settle down.

"Now you wait here for a minute and let me get Jake. You'll see everything is okay. You just have to be more careful about going up to him while he's eating. Okay?"

"Don't bring him in here!" Bubba insisted, starting to cry all over again.

"Stop being silly. Wait here. You don't have to pat him if you don't want to."

Brenda went back to the kitchen. Jake had finished eating and was standing by the glass doors looking out into the yard.

"Come, Jake," Brenda called.

He came over immediately. Brenda took him out to the living room where both kids sat on the couch. Bubba lifted his feet up, howling. Brenda shook her head.

"Jake's not going to hurt you," she told him.

She sat down on the floor and patted the floor for Jake to lie down. He lay down and turned over to show his belly for her to scratch. She scratched his belly and his ears. After a few minutes, the children started to calm down. Brenda kept patting Jake and giving him attention. Eventually, Bubba jumped down from the couch.

"Can I pat him?" he asked.

"Of course. Come on over."

He came over, and Brenda pulled him into her lap, and helped him hold his hand out to Jake, and then to pat Jake gently.

"See? Jakey's fine. You just scared him. He won't hurt you."

Sniffling, Bubba nodded. "It's okay," he agreed.

CHAPTER FIVE

Barry watched the two cocker spaniels race wildly around the yard playing with each other. They acted like puppies instead of grown dogs. He smiled, smoking his pipe, and sat down in his rocking chair for some fresh air. He closed his eyes as the sun shone on his face, and without realizing it, he drifted off to sleep.

Sharon woke him when she got back from the grocery store.

"Barry! Barry, wake up!"

Barry startled, snorted, and sat up straight. He looked around. The light in the yard was growing dim. The dogs were no longer chasing each other around, but were lying companionably side by side on the porch beside him, quiet and calm.

"Hi honey," he said, pushing himself up to his feet.

Sharon bent over and picked up his pipe.

"You want to set the house on fire? Falling asleep while smoking your pipe?"

"I put it out before I took my nap," Barry lied, taking it back from her. "And nobody ever burned down a house with a pipe. Only with cigars and cigarettes.

"You shouldn't even be smoking. You know what the doctor said."

Barry shrugged. "I know the doctor doesn't want me to have any fun.

No smoking, no drinking, no sugar, no steak. He takes all the fun out of living to an old age. Who wants to live like that?"

"With your diabetes—"

"I know, I know. I wasn't worried about it before I got diabetes, and I'm not worried about it now. When the Lord calls me, I'll go. But it's not my time."

"That doesn't mean you have to go trying risky behaviors," she scolded.

"I'm not skydiving, darling. I had my fill of risky behaviors when I was a youngster. Now I'm just sitting in my rocker watching my dogs. Nothing risky."

"Except you're trying to burn down the house with your pipe."

Barry shook his head.

"Nobody ever burned down the house with a pipe. Now are you going to make me some supper, now you got some groceries?"

"Don't I always?"

"I want red meat, no chicken breasts," he warned.

Sharon rolled her eyes.

"The doctor said—"

"The doctor said a little red meat now and then is fine. It doesn't have to be a twelve-ounce steak, darling. Just a taste. You can even mix it up with those dang vegetables you're always stirring. As long as it's got steak in it, I'll eat it without complaining."

Sharon smiled and laughed at him.

"I'll make you some stir fry," she promised.

"As long as I can put soy sauce on it," Barry amended.

"You can put soy sauce on it."

"Not that reduced-salt crap."

"That's all we've got," Sharon said with a shrug.

Barry sighed. They went into the house, and Barry started to unload the groceries while Sharon busied herself getting the stove ready, and a few dishes washed up and out of the way.

"White rice, not brown stuff," Barry told her.

"It's half-and-half."

"Can't you make me white rice?"

"I did. And brown rice. And mixed them together."

"It takes three times as long to make it that way."

"But you eat it," she teased.

Barry chuckled. There was a scratching at the door, and he went to let the dogs in. "Come on in girls! Did you get tired of playing outside?"

Sharon shook her head at him. "I swear, you give them more attention than you did your own kids."

Barry washed their paws gently before letting them the rest of the way into the house. Then he looked at Sharon.

"They smell better than the kids," he joked. "And they're better behaved."

He changed their water dishes and topped off their food bowls. As they started to eat, he patted their heads.

"There you go, girls. You played hard; you eat up."

———

Barry struggled to make it up the stairs. It was getting harder and harder each day. It was time to find a house where it was easier to get around. Maybe a condo, so someone else could take care of the yard, too. He was just getting too old for it.

He stopped for a rest halfway up the stairs, breathing heavily. The girls ran up and down the stairs, waiting for him to finish the journey to the top. Sharon was getting ready for bed. He heard her turn off the water and put her toothbrush in the jar.

"Barry, are you okay?" she called from the bedroom.

"Yes, I'll be up in a minute," he told her.

He waited for a few more breaths and then started up the stairs again. When he got to the top, he rested again. The girls followed him, more sedate now.

"What's taking so long?" Sharon asked. She looked at him. "Are you okay? You're flushed."

"Just getting a bit harder to get up the stairs. I'm tired today."

"You need to stop smoking and lose weight," she admonished.

"Not today," Barry sighed.

He went to brush his own teeth and perform his other oblations. When he got out of the bathroom, the girls were waiting patiently for him on the other side of the door. He patted each of them and led them over to their beds.

"A treat before bed," he told them, and he got out a tooth-cleaning biscuit for each one of them. As they settled on their beds, he gave them each their biscuit, patted them once more on the head and scratched their ears. Then he climbed into bed with Sharon and settled in.

"Love you, sweetie," he told her, giving her a hug and kiss. She turned off the light.

When Barry started to snore, the two small dogs climbed up on the bed and nestled into the space beside him.

———

Sharon awoke and stretched, forcing her eyes open. She sat up, and looked down at her sleeping husband, gazing at his peaceful face. She pushed at the dogs with her toes.

"Get off the bed," she murmured. "Go on. Go to your beds."

They looked at her with their liquid brown eyes and didn't move. They panted, tongues out in doggie smiles. They were warm and comfortable, and there was no way they were moving at her whispered command. Barry shifted in his sleep, wheezing a bit, and settling again. Sharon drew circles on the soft skin of his inner arm.

"Barry. Time to wake up," she told him.

Barry's eyes squinted open and he smiled at her. "Morning, sweetheart," he said hoarsely.

"How was your night?"

He shrugged. "Restless, but okay." He yawned. "How about yours?"

"The girls woke me up a few times."

He shifted his legs and looked down at the dogs. "Goldie and Gilda," he reproached. "Why aren't you in your beds?"

They both looked at him panting happily. After a moment, they both stood up and came over to snuffle at his hands and lick his face. Barry laughed.

"They say they're sorry for keeping you awake," he told Sharon.

She laughed. "They do not! You spoil those girls rotten," she said.

"I know. But they're so sweet."

"You can't keep letting them sleep on the bed with you, you know."

"Eh," he grunted. "It doesn't bother me."

"But they keep you from getting a good sleep too. Not just me."

Barry shifted and swung his feet over the side of the bed. He rubbed his swollen legs. "Old bones," he complained. "Why do we have to keep getting older, Sharon?"

"I don't know why *you* have to keep getting older. *I'm* certainly not."

He looked at her. She had gray hair and lots of wrinkles pointing cheerfully up. She was still lithe and shapely. A bit slower, but faster than he was. Her smile was still girlish and could set his heart racing. Or maybe his heart just raced a lot more as he got older.

"You're still as beautiful as the day I met you," he confirmed.

"I know I don't feel any older. I always thought old people must feel as old as they look. But I still feel like a twenty-year-old in my head. What kind of dirty trick is that?"

Barry nodded.

"They never told us our bodies would get older, but we'd still feel like kids. I don't feel mature, or confident. I thought I was going to know everything by now."

"And life still surprises us. Well, at least it's not boring."

"Things could be worse," Barry admitted, and he bent over to kiss her.

The dogs tried to push between them. Barry finished the kiss and then scratched their heads.

"Come on, girls; I'll take you outside."

They jumped down off of the bed eagerly and led the way down the stairs. Barry pulled on his robe and made his way down the stairs. His knees cracked and ached, but he knew they'd feel better as he moved around and warmed them up. He let the dogs out and turned on the coffee maker. While he waited, he browsed through the fridge for anything good. He cut off a chunk of cheese and nibbled at it while he watched the dogs out the window. Sharon wasn't down yet, and when the dogs came back in, he broke off a little bit of cheese for each of them and fed them.

"Don't you tell Momma," he warned them.

"Don't tell me what?" Sharon asked, sneaking down the stairs with a tread like a cat's. "What are you feeding those dogs now?"

Barry popped the rest of the cheese in his mouth.

"Nothing," he said, talking around it as he chewed.

"Barry Munsch, you are incorrigible!" she accused.

"I know, baby. But then, you always were attracted to the bad boys."

Sharon walked over to the coffee machine and poured them each a cup.

"Put a pinch of sugar in mine?" Barry suggested.

"No sugar. You checked your levels this morning?"

"No, not yet."

"Well, get to it before you eat anything else. We need to know how much insulin you need."

Barry rolled his eyes. "Just let me feed the girls first."

"You need to look after yourself before the dogs. The girls will be fine."

CHAPTER SIX

Brenda was out in the garden enjoying the weather. The cool fall air was refreshing. Cool enough to need a sweater, but not so much she needed gloves or a hat. There wouldn't be a lot of nice days left before the snow flew, and then there would be no more gardening until the spring.

She pulled the last of the carrots and turned to the potato patch. She looked at her watch to see how much time she had before she would need to get lunch together for the kids. They were playing in the sandbox. But before long, she'd have to feed them and get them ready for preschool.

Brenda grabbed the shovel from the shed and started to dig the potatoes. There was something dark in the corner of the potato patch and Brenda went to pick up whatever garbage had blown in. Her hand was about an inch away when she realized it was furry. It was a black animal, not a garbage bag or piece of trash. She gasped and stared at the stiff body. At first, she thought it was another squirrel. But as she stared, trying to sort out the shadows and shapes, she realized it was a cat. Uggh. Was it the neighbor's cat? Had it been poisoned or caught its neck on something?

Getting closer, she realized that it had been no accident. The catch had been savaged; ripped apart.

Brenda glanced over at the kids playing in the sandbox. She couldn't do anything to draw their attention to the poor deceased beast. She'd have to leave it until after they were at preschool. Until then, she needed to keep them out of the area.

"Kids, let's go in the house and make some cookies," Brenda called.

Getting them out of the sandbox before it was time could prove to be a difficult prospect. But if they had an incentive… cookie making was a rare treat. Brenda could make some peanut butter cookies. It was a simple, three-ingredient recipe. Pretty much foolproof, other than preventing the kids from eating dough with raw egg in it.

The children looked up and then looked at each other. With big smiles, they jumped up and ran toward her, sandy hands and faces.

"No, go straight into the house, not over here!" Brenda warned them. "Brush off on the mat."

They turned around and buzzed to the door, where they brushed themselves off half-heartedly and then stomped into the house, leaving a fine layer of play sand in the entryway.

"Take off your shoes," Brenda instructed, coming up behind them. "They're full of sand."

Bubba had his off first. Cassy whined and begged for help. Brenda bent down, wiping her sweaty face with the back of her hand. She helped Cassy to get her shoes undone and off her feet.

"There you go. Now you guys go wash your hands. Right now," Brenda motioned to the bathroom beside the kitchen.

They headed off, bickering over the sink and spraying each other. They came back with not just their hands, but also their faces dripping. Brenda smiled, shaking her head. She looked around.

"Where's Jake?"

"Him sleeping," Cassy advised, motioning to the front room.

Brenda went in and found him sleeping on the couch. Not on his bed, but in Darren's spot.

"Jake!" Brenda snapped.

His eyes flew open and his head popped up. But he didn't get off the couch.

"Get down!" Brenda shouted. "Down off the couch!"

He looked at her for a moment and then slid off the front of the couch, oozing from the seat cushion to the floor. He sat down, head hanging low, his ears and tail hanging motionless.

"Come to your kennel," Brenda told him. He didn't move. "Come!" Brenda insisted.

The dog heeled, his head still down, acting like she had beaten him. Brenda took him past the kids in the kitchen and pointed at his open kennel.

"In your kennel," she ordered.

He obeyed her slowly; his hangdog look not missed by the kids.

"Mama," Cassy whined. "Why go bed?"

"He didn't do anything wrong," Bubba protested. "Now he's sad."

"He'll be just fine. You don't want him jumping up trying to eat your cookies, do you?"

Bubba laughed. "Yes, I do! That would be funny!"

Cassy joined in on the giggles. Brenda rolled her eyes.

"Well, I don't want him jumping up trying to eat your cookies. Eww, dog germs."

In his cage, Jake whined, the noise becoming more and more high-pitched and hard to ignore.

"Jake! Shut up!" Brenda shouted.

He stopped whining. Brenda gathered together the ingredients for the peanut butter cookies. The excited kids forgot all about poor Jake, eager to help to mix and form the balls to make the cookies. When they were done, the cookie sheet was covered with varying shapes and thicknesses of what would have to be called cookies. But they bore little resemblance to the ones she bought at the bakery or grocery store. Brenda slid them into the oven, looking at the clock.

"Okay. It's time for lunch. Let's get some sandwiches, and when you're done, the cookies will be ready to eat!"

They both cheered.

———

After Brenda had dropped the kids off at preschool, she let Jake out of his kennel. She shook her head at his whining and yelping.

"You'd think I was killing you! Dogs are supposed to like their kennels. They're like nice warm caves. Didn't you know that? Don't you like your nice warm cave?"

Jake nuzzled her hand. Brenda patted him and rubbed his ears, looking into his face.

"Why did you do that?" she asked. "You get lots to eat. Lots of time to play and exercise. I can't understand why you'd have to kill things."

But she did understand. She had just finished pointing out the dog's resemblance to its ancestor, the wolf. Did a wolf stop killing if it was fed regularly? Somehow, it didn't seem likely. And the dog was a wolf. He had genetic memory. Instinct. He did what wolves do.

Darn the neighbors for letting their cat run outside free instead of keeping it indoors. Cats did just fine kept inside instead of being let out to wander. They should have taken care of it properly.

Brenda went upstairs and looked in at Erin. The baby slept peacefully, looking like a little angel. Brenda stroked her hair very softly, careful not to wake her, and went back downstairs. She got out a garbage bag and headed out to the yard to clean up the mess. She attempted to pick up the body of the cat like she would Jake's droppings, turning the bag partly inside out, grabbing it through the bag. The trouble was, the little corpse was torn up, not in one piece, but nearly decapitated, belly ripped open and bowels spilling out when she tried to lift it into the bag. Brenda gagged, her stomach heaved, dangerously close to losing her lunch. She steeled herself, giving herself a tough pep talk.

You can do this. You've seen dead things before. It's not your fault, but it is your dog, and you have to clean up your dog's messes. Two minutes, and it will all be done.

Just grab whatever you can through the bag. Just scoop it all in. Don't look at it. Don't smell.

Just push it all into the bag, and tie the bag up.

Brenda was just finishing up when Erin started screaming. Not just an 'I woke up' cry, but a horrifying shriek of pain. Brenda jumped up and ran into the house. Her feet barely touched the stairs. She raced up to the crib, but before she got to Erin's room, she was confronted with a terrible sight. Jake was in the hallway. He had Erin. There was blood everywhere. Erin was no longer screaming or even moving; she was limp in his jaws.

"Jake, drop her!" Brenda screamed.

Jake didn't. He crouched in front of her, growling. But no growl was going to stop Brenda today. Without hesitation, she charged him and hit him on the top of his skull hard with her closed fist.

"Drop her! Drop her! Let go!"

The dog snapped at her. Brenda hit him again.

"No! No, no, no! Not my baby!"

He let go of the baby to bite her. His jaws clamped over her arm, and with the other hand, Brenda grabbed Erin and cuddled her against her body, tears streaming down her face. She twisted and wrenched her arm away from Jake, kicking him, screaming and growling at him incoherently. She was an animal herself, beyond being able to reason or give him a command.

"My baby, my baby," Brenda wept, now holding Erin with both hands, searching for some sign of life. The dog's teeth had lacerated Erin's scalp, and must have pierced her belly as well. There was blood soaking through the sleeper and blood dripping down her face.

Brenda kicked the horrible beast into Erin's room and slammed the door. She put Erin on the floor and bent over, listening for her breath. There was no sign of life. Brenda swore and cried, her brain in a frenzy, unable to focus and decide what to do. Tears flowed down her face.

Nine-one-one. Call nine-one-one.

Brenda fumbled for her phone and flipped it open. With shaking fingers, she dialed. First, she got the cell provider emergency operator, asking her for her location and what service she wanted. Brenda sobbed, asking for an ambulance.

"My baby was bit by a dog," she explained.

"Is she bleeding?"

"Yes!"

"Is she still conscious? Breathing?"

"No. No, she's not. I don't know what to do."

"Do you know CPR?"

"No… yes… I don't know…"

The operator walked her through performing CPR on the infant. In a daze, Brenda tried to obey, tried to get Erin breathing, to get her heart beating. All the while, hot tears ran down her face, and she sobbed, willing Erin to breathe.

"Come on, baby, come on. Erin. Breathe. Breathe, baby, please…"

———

She heard the ambulance pull in front of the house and stopped the CPR. She picked Erin up and raced downstairs to unlock the door and hand her to the paramedic.

"Please, do something," she begged.

The paramedic examined Erin. Placing her on the floor, he went to work. Brenda hung on every move. He was so slow. Erin made no movement or sound. The second paramedic asked her questions, and Brenda answered the best she could. But she was so confused and so worried about Erin. A second ambulance arrived. A police car. Another police car. Brenda didn't understand why they were all there. One of the policemen took her by the arm and led her into the kitchen to talk to her.

"No," Brenda resisted being taken out of sight of Erin. "No, I have to stay with her."

"Let the medics do their job," he told her, and firmly pulled her out of the room.

Brenda wiped at the tears on her face. "She's going to be okay," she insisted. "Tell me she's going to be okay."

"Mrs. Brooks. The baby is dead."

"No!" Brenda shrieked. "No, she can't be dead!"

"Why don't you tell me what happened?"

Brenda tried to describe the sequence of events. Her whole body was shaking. She looked down at her hands to see them covered with blood. Erin's blood. But Brenda was injured too. Her arm was ripped and bleeding, savagely bitten. The policeman followed her eyes.

"We'd better get that looked at," he said. "You're going to need stitches and maybe shots. Where is the dog now?"

"He's… upstairs. I shut him in Erin's room."

The cop took a moment to talk to someone on his radio to direct animal control upstairs to get Jake.

Brenda sat down on one of the kitchen stools, tears coursing down her cheeks, trying to regain control.

"What am I going to do?" she sobbed. "I don't know what to do!"

"Just try to settle down. Has the dog ever bitten anyone before?"

"We haven't had him for very long. We got him at the pound."

"We'll follow up with them to check his previous history. Did you ask about his previous history?"

"They said he had lived with a retired couple. That he was just fine. They said he'd be okay with kids!"

"Uh-huh. And he hadn't bitten anyone while you had him?"

"No—just—no."

There was a pause.

"Just what?" the cop asked, studying her shrewdly.

"He snapped at Bubba the other day. Bubba ran in when Jake was eating. He was just too close to his food. But Jake didn't bite Bubba. He just snapped and growled."

The officer wrote something down in his notepad, slowly, painstakingly, with a tiny pencil pinched between his fingers so awkwardly it must have been painful to write.

"Uh-huh," the officer acknowledged. "And he hasn't bitten or threatened to bite anyone else?"

"No. Never. He's been very shy and quiet. He likes me to scratch his belly. I don't understand what happened. He was down here; the baby was all the way upstairs in her crib. Why would he even go up there?"

"He's never shown any interest in the baby before?"

"Not really, no."

"Not really?"

"Well, we introduced them, you know. Showed her to him. He was fine with it. Didn't growl or anything."

"I see. What were you doing when the attack occurred? Where were you?"

"I was outside, cleaning up the—the garden."

She looked toward the garden. The officer glanced at the back yard through the sliding doors and nodded.

"So how long was he alone with the baby?"

"He wasn't with the baby. He was in a completely different part of the house."

"How long was he in the house with her while you were outside?"

"I don't know. Just a few minutes. It wasn't long."

"You have other kids, Mrs. Brooks?" he asked, looking around the kitchen.

"Yes, a boy and a girl. They are four and two."

"And where are they right now?"

"At preschool. I need to pick them up soon."

"We'll have to arrange for someone else to pick them up. Is there a friend you can call?"

"Umm—we're new to the neighborhood. I don't know a lot of people yet. I should call Darren. He can pick them up."

"We don't want Mr. Brooks driving after hearing his baby has been killed," the cop said sensibly. "He can meet them here. If you don't have anyone who can pick them up, we can send an officer over."

Brenda nodded. "Okay. Yes, I guess so."

"Have you had a dog before, Mrs. Brooks?"

"Yes. I grew up around dogs. I never even heard of a dog doing something like this! Could he be rabid? I can't understand it!"

"We'll do a rabies test to be sure. You'll need shots if he is. You've never had another dog that showed violent tendencies?"

"No. Never. Our dogs were always very gentle. It doesn't make any sense. He was such a wuss; I can't understand him doing something like this. Why would he go into Erin's room? Why would he take her out of the bed?"

"Some dogs are predatory," the officer said. "It is in their natures. Some dogs just never shake the instinct to hunt."

Brenda shuddered. The cop went over to the pegs on the wall and pulled off one of her coats.

"Just put that around you," he suggested, draping it around her shoulders. "You can't put it all the way on until your arm has been looked at, but for now, it will keep you a bit warmer."

"I'm not cold," Brenda objected.

"You're in shock."

"Where is Erin?" Brenda asked, making a move to go back out to the living room. "I need to see her."

"Not right now. The medics will look after the body until the coroner gets a chance to get here. Your family will get her body back after the investigation."

"Investigation," Brenda repeated blankly. "What investigation?"

"A child has been killed, ma'am. We need to investigate."

"But it was the dog. You know it was the dog. What do you need to investigate?"

"The circumstances surrounding the dog killing her," he said obliquely.

Brenda frowned and shook her head. "I don't know what you mean," she said.

"Just let me take care of it. It's all right."

"Well, what am I going to do? I can't just sit here."

"No. First, let's get one of the paramedics to take a look at your arm and get you stitched up."

He spoke to the unseen person on his radio again, and in a few minutes, one of the paramedics entered the kitchen with his equipment case.

"Let's have a look, shall we?" he offered, approaching Brenda.

He put on a pair of blue gloves and took Brenda's arms, looking at them closely.

"Well, that's nasty, isn't it? We'll need a doctor to suture it, but for now, let's at least get it cleaned up and covered. Doesn't look like it's bleeding too badly anymore. Missed the arteries."

Brenda sat there numbly as he rifled through his kit to pull out wipes, antiseptic, and white bandages. She sat and watched him tape and bandage her up temporarily until they could get to the hospital for the doctor to look at her.

———

After putting Brenda Brooks in a squad car headed for the hospital, Carter took a slow look around the house, mulling over the details. He went over to the dog control van and looked into the cage at the dog in question. It was a large dog, medium brown, with a muzzle too sharp for a pure retriever. A muzzle now covered with blood. When Carter peered into the cage, the dog put its head down, ears sagging, and rolled his eyes back.

"Does he look like a killer?" Carter asked the dog control guy, with a name badge that said Pete.

"You can never tell," Pete said with an expressive shrug. "He's a big dog, so he's physically capable. You get a toy and they may bite, but they're not going to kill anyone, even a baby. But he's big enough. He may not act vicious, but you can never tell."

"He hasn't growled or acted vicious with you?"

"No, came quiet as a lamb."

"I would never have pegged that one as a killer. Anything I should be asking about with his history?"

"Just about any bites in the past. I doubt if you'll find anything, though. Any shelter will put down a dog with a biting history rather than put him out for adoption."

Carter nodded. "Okay."

He went back into the house and up the stairs to the scene of the crime. There was blood spatter everywhere in the hallway and the doorway of the baby's bedroom. Between the baby and Mrs. Brooks, a lot of blood had been shed and sprayed around. There wasn't much else he could tell from the scene. The crib was tipped over. She had been telling the truth about the baby having been in the crib. But what had driven the dog to go after the baby? It was such a bizarre situation.

Back down the stairs, Carter looked around the kitchen, but there was nothing enlightening there. He gazed out the window at the back yard. Mrs. Brooks had been reticent about what she had been doing in the back yard. Carter slid open the porch doors and went for a look around.

She had been pulling vegetables; there was a pile of carrots to the side. And some weeds had been pulled. The children's sandbox was uncovered. There was a garbage bag over by the potato patch. He went over to look at the garbage bag. Pulling weeds there too? But no… the garbage bag held a surprise. Carter looked for a few minutes and then went back into the house. He walked through to the front of the house again and looked to see if Pete was still there. Pete was, hanging around to see if anyone needed him any further.

"There's a dead cat in the back yard," Carter told him, without introduction.

Pete chewed on his gum for a few minutes, considering.

"Look like it was killed by a dog?" he asked.

Carter nodded. "Torn up pretty thoroughly. Can't tell how much he might have eaten, and how much was just the sport."

More chewing, more thinking. "Maybe," Pete conceded. "Dogs that have been killing other animals… it might be a sign they are vicious… I know of dogs that have attacked humans, with a history of attacking or killing other dogs or animals. I don't know what the psychology is, but the animal obviously doesn't have the proper discipline."

Carter nodded. "Thanks. If you have any research to back that up, I'd appreciate you sending it my way, okay?"

"Sure. I'll look it up."

Carter went back into the house for a last look around. What he didn't do was go back to look at the baby at rest in the ambulance. The sight was already impressed on his memory. The poor little thing, head lacerated, bites across the torso, hands, and legs. There was a lot of bleeding; the baby obviously hadn't died immediately. The bites were savage. Not just an accidental bite; that dog had meant to kill her.

———

Brenda had been pampered and cared for at the hospital by doctors and nurses with kind, gentle eyes. Everyone looked at her with sympathy, exclaimed at the vicious bites on her arm, and tried to comfort her. The tears had stopped and Brenda felt drained, squeezed out, emotionless. Eventually, the policeman who had kindly stayed with her was joined by Carter, the one who had first talked to her at the house.

"How are you doing, Mrs. Brooks?" he asked.

"I'm all taken care of, if that's what you mean."

"Good. How are you feeling?"

Brenda shook her head heavily. "How would *you* feel?" she asked. "I can't believe this is happening. How could this happen?"

"I'm very sorry for your loss."

She just shook her head. "It's crazy. I don't understand why he would attack the baby. Is he rabid?"

"We talked about that before. We will have him tested to find out. You haven't noticed any violence or problems with discipline?" he prodded.

"No."

"Except for snapping at your son."

"That was just one time," Brenda protested. "Just when Bubba got to close to his food. Any dog would do that."

"He never snapped at anyone else?"

Brenda sighed. "I don't know," she said in frustration.

"You don't know. So he might have."

"I guess. I didn't notice anything out of the ordinary. I've had dogs before. He seemed perfectly normal. Just a wuss, a little shy."

"Why don't you tell me about the cat?"

Brenda looked at his face, stunned. How did he know about the cat? He looked back at her steadily, waiting for a response. What was she supposed to say?

"I don't know," Brenda said carefully. "I just found it in the back yard today. I don't know how it got there or what happened to it."

"It was attacked by an animal."

"That's what it looked like. But… it could be a coyote… They do find their way into the city. We're close to the greenway. Maybe it was a coyote. Or a cougar."

"Or maybe it was the animal that was supposed to be in the yard. You didn't notice anything unusual? Didn't hear a fight or the dog barking?"

"No… dogs bark all the time. Or chase birds or squirrels because they're bored. It doesn't mean anything. I never heard him fighting with the cat."

"But you've heard him barking or growling in the back yard. So he could have."

"Yes, of course, he could have. But why would he? Most dogs will just chase a cat back over the fence. They think it's fun. It's a game."

"For this dog, it wasn't a game, though, was it? Does your husband take him hunting?"

"No. No, my husband doesn't hunt."

"And you've never noticed any… stalking behavior? Toward animals, or children, or anyone?"

"No! He's—he's a good dog," Brenda insisted.

The cop's eyes searching her face intently. Brenda looked away, sure he could detect her small fib.

"Mrs. Brooks, you need to be honest with me," he advised. "It is important."

Brenda nodded. "Yes."

"I don't think you're telling the truth. Has he stalked one of the children before? And maybe you just thought it was cute behavior? A game?"

"No. No, he never acted threatening toward the children."

"What about toward other animals? You ever see him chase a cat? Hunt a duck? What?"

Brenda felt sick. "A squirrel," she admitted. "He… stalked it… crept up on it and then killed it."

"So you do know he's capable of intentionally killing another animal. You don't think he did the same to the cat? Just because most dogs will chase a cat over the fence willy-nilly, that doesn't mean they can't sneak up on it, take it by surprise, just like he did the squirrel."

Brenda put her face in her hands, shaking her head. "Yes, I suppose he could have. Of course, he could have. But that doesn't mean he did. There's no proof he killed the cat. It could have been a wild animal that got into the yard."

"Well, it's certainly more likely the cat got into the yard and was killed by your dog than a cat and a wild animal both got into the yard at the same time."

Brenda shrugged helplessly. "Okay, yes. It was probably him. It was more likely him. But that doesn't explain why he would go after Erin. She was sleeping in her crib. She's not a wild animal. She's not in his territory. Why would he go after her for no reason?"

Carter shrugged. "I'm no expert in animal psychology. But it seems to me if he stalked and killed a squirrel, and stalked and killed a cat, he's not just defending his territory, he's hunting. And the baby was a small, help-less prey."

"But they weren't even in the same room!"

"That didn't stop him. He knew she was in the house. He could hear or smell her. He knew from experience where she slept, and she was help-less to run away or defend herself. All he needed was the opportunity. You gave him free run of the house, with the baby unguarded. He just needed the opportunity, and you provided it."

"You make it sound like it's my fault!" Brenda objected. "I would never have left him in the house if I thought he was a danger to my family!"

"Perhaps you should have thought about it. Perhaps three warnings should have been enough to make you more careful."

Brenda's mouth hung open and she tried to think of what to say. She shook her head. "What are you saying? You're saying it is my fault?"

The officer looked at her, taking a deep breath and letting it out slow-ly. "I'm putting you under arrest for manslaughter."

"What?"

"I'm putting—"

"You think I killed my baby?" Brenda demanded. "The dog killed her! It was unprovoked! I didn't kill my own baby! Just look at me!" She held out her bandaged arms toward him. "I did everything I could to protect her! I tried!"

"You were negligent in allowing a dangerous animal access to her. You left her unsupervised. You left the dog free to roam the house. You knew he had snapped at the children and had hunted other animals. You should have been more careful."

He came up to her and put a handcuff over one bandaged arm. He turned her around and put the other handcuff over her other arm.

Brenda let him, overwhelmed and confused. How could it be happening? It was all some horrible mistake. How could they do this? She had to talk to Darren. Darren would sort it out, would make sense of it and make the police behave in a reasonable way.

She couldn't be arrested and sent to jail.

———

Brenda was relieved when finally Darren came by to see her. She had been through hell being arrested, booked, questioned, and jailed. It felt like it would never end.

"Darren!"

She reached out to hug him, but he stepped back, rebuffing her. He brushed her arms aside.

"I can't believe you did this," Darren accused.

Brenda was floored. "*I* did this? I did *what?* What are you talking about?"

Darren looked at her shaking his head. "What am I talking about? My baby is dead, Brenda. How could you leave the dog alone in the house with her? How could you let him be around the kids like that?"

"You know Jake. He wasn't a vicious dog. He wasn't dangerous. I didn't have any idea he would go after Erin. How could I know that?"

"The cop told me about the squirrel and the cat and about him snapping at Bubba. You should have known."

"How could I know? I never saw any indication he was going to hurt Erin. He never acted that way toward any of the kids."

"He tried to bite Bubba."

"He just snapped. It wasn't anything. Bubba wasn't in any danger."

"Bubba was scared."

Brenda looked for an argument. "He was startled…"

"Both kids were crying, Brenda."

"You knew that, and you never said we should keep Jake away from them. Nobody ever thought he was dangerous."

"Getting a dog was your idea," Darren snapped.

"You said it was okay. You were on board with it. You helped me pick him out!"

"It was your decision. I couldn't care less which dog you picked out. But I thought you would pick a safe dog. You said you were going to pick a good family dog. A good dog that could grow up with the kids. You said he'd be good with them."

"I tried, Darren," Brenda said, her eyes burning, and a hot lump rising in her throat. "I tried to pick a good dog, a good family dog. I thought Jake would be good for the kids."

"You were wrong," Darren snapped. "It's your fault."

"No, it's not my fault! I didn't know! The guy at the pound said he'd be good with kids. He said he'd never had any problems. He said he'd be a good family dog. You can't blame me. Darren, please."

"It's over, Brenda. My baby's gone. You're dead to me. Now it's just me, and Bubba, and Cassy. Now I'm a single dad and have to figure out how to raise them all by myself. Is that fair to them? You destroyed the family. Completely ripped it apart. So stupid and careless. How could you ruin our family over a dog?"

"I didn't know! I just found the cat today. I didn't know it was Jake. I didn't know he'd go after the baby. If I ever thought he'd go after the baby, I wouldn't have left them in the house together. I promise you. I wouldn't risk my kids for a dog."

"Well, you did. And you were wrong."

"Don't leave me, Darren. Don't abandon me. You promised 'for better or worse.' Please don't leave me here to fend for myself. I need help. I need someone on my side. I'm going to need a lawyer, and money, and… I don't even know. I can't do it on my own, Darren. Please. Just say you'll think about it. You don't have to say yes or no. Just think about it."

Darren shook his head. "It's over, Brenda. It's all over. When I said for better or worse, I never envisioned anything like this. This is impossible. No one could have imagined anything like this. There's no way I could stay with you. There's no way I could stand for this, say I still loved you and supported you and wanted to stand by you. How could I do that, when you killed my baby?"

Brenda buried her face in her hands. "No, Darren. Don't take everything away from me."

"You just took everything away from me."

He turned around and went to the door. He signaled to the policeman standing on the other side. The cop opened the door and let Darren out.

CHAPTER SEVEN

Frank was headed for his favorite cafe for lunch after signing himself out on his radio. He stopped on the sidewalk outside the cafe as a man with a dog stopped right in front of him, waiting for his pooch to do his business. Frank was disgusted—in the middle of the city sidewalk! Did people have no sense of shame? It was a big dog, and the pile of crap it deposited in front of Frank stank to high heaven. Frank frowned fiercely, trying to keep the memories at bay. But he smelled again the inside of the trailer, the feces and urine and the smell of decomposing bodies. It made him want to vomit right there.

The owner of the dog started to move on.

"Pick up after your dog," Frank growled at him, angry at his disregard for others. He was angrier at the flashback, the memory of the bloody muzzles of the crazed dogs, all coming toward him.

The man turned around with a sneer on his face, but when he saw Frank's uniform, his expression quickly turned to one of subservience.

"Of course, officer. Of course, I will," he agreed. He didn't want to get a fine. He dug around in his pockets to find a plastic bag, obviously used to simply walking away from his dog's deposits whenever there wasn't a cop around. He picked up the mess the best he could, shrugging at Frank nervously about the smear left on the sidewalk, his eyes a little afraid.

"Curb him next time," Frank said. "Don't let him do his business in the middle of the sidewalk."

The dog started to bark at Frank, not liking his angry tone. The man pulled him back and tried to shut him up.

"Of course," he agreed. "I'll make sure next time."

He turned tail and left, tugging the barking dog behind him.

Frank leaned on the wall of the building next to him, taking deep breaths, trying to wipe out the smell of the dog crap and the crazy barking echoing in his head. How was he ever going to hear another dog bark again without seeing and hearing those murderous brutes straining at him, their faces dark with blood? He breathed, and swallowed, and eventually managed to peel himself away from the wall and enter the cafe.

A nice bowl of soup and a few minutes to rest and compose his thoughts, and he would be fine.

———

The soup of the day was a butternut squash. Not very macho, but Frank loved it anyway. It made him think of Halloween and Elsie trick-or-treating in her latest costume—a princess, or a ballerina, usually something girlie and frilly. But there had been a few years of witches or punk rockers, too. A nice hot soup on a cold night, the bright stars in the chilly, dark sky. It soothed his soul, settled him back down again. The anxiety created by the incident with the dog out front seeped away, and he started to feel like himself again.

Frank watched the news on the TV above the counter. All political and boring, nothing of any real interest. Weather reports, cold fronts moving in and out. Some community events coming up. A slow news day. But then they switched to national news, and Frank watched footage of officers escorting a young mother into a police station. She was clean cut, good looking, not a junkie or hooker. What had she gotten herself into? A zoom-in showed white bandages wrapped around her arms, and a red, tear-swollen face. Frank frowned, watching carefully. The sound was turned down, but closed captioning was on, and Frank tried to watch the words and the picture at the same time.

"Twenty-seven-year-old Brenda Brooks was arrested this afternoon for manslaughter, after leaving her infant daughter alone with the family dog. She was doing yard work outside, and when she returned to the house to check on her daughter, she was shocked to find it had been savagely killed by the dog."

The soup was suddenly a solid lump in Frank's stomach and he felt dangerously sick. The spoon clattered from his hand. It was a coincidence. There were dog bites and dog killings every year. There was no relationship to the Johnsons. This incident was halfway across the country.

"Police say the dog was known to be vicious," the reporter added. "The accused has two other young children."

It's not related, Frank scolded himself. It was not one of the Johnson dogs. She might look responsible and put together, but despite her looks, she was a careless mother. A mother who cared less about the safety of her children than her own comfort. Who had for some unfathomable reason, kept a vicious dog in the house, unsupervised, putting her child at risk.

Maybe she was a drug dealer and the dog was there to guard her stash. It was a good thing they got her off the streets. And the dog would be destroyed. Unlike the Johnson's dogs, which nobody believed would offend again, after killing an infant this dog would be put down and would never be a danger to anyone again.

This case was different. They knew what the dog had done. It had attacked and killed a child. There was no question. And the dog would be put down, so it could never harm anyone again.

———

That night, Frank sat back from the table, pushing his plate away slightly and giving Janice a satisfied smile.

"I'm stuffed. That was great, honey. You know I'm going to have to go for a long run to work it off now…"

Janice smiled back. "It's not like you have been gaining weight lately. If anything, you've lost weight. You need a chance just to relax and do something for yourself."

"I've just been stressed," he sighed. "It's hard not to be… I don't want to keep obsessing, but it just gets into my head, worms its way in and I can't get it out." He rubbed his temples.

"It's all over now. Why don't you work on your trains? You need something to distract yourself. So you're not depressed about it all the time."

Frank nodded. "I know," he agreed. "It's just so hard to focus, even on the trains. Did you see the news?" he asked. "About the dog that killed a baby down south?"

Janice shook her head. "How awful," she exclaimed. She started to clear the dishes. "Do you want to get some ice cream out for dessert?"

"No, I've had too much to eat already. It was just a baby, Janice. Mom apparently left it alone with the dog. So tragic."

"Do you know if the electrical bill got paid last month?" Janice asked, desperately trying to derail his train of thought. "There was a balance forward on the bill."

"I'm sure it got paid. Maybe it was just a day late." Frank got up from the table and headed straight for the TV. "News should be on in a minute. We'll see if they say anything else about the baby."

"You don't want to watch it, Frank. It will just keep you up all night. Let's play Scrabble."

"I'll just watch for a minute. It might not even be on. There are dog bites and killings all the time; they don't usually make it to the news. It probably won't be on again."

"But..."

It was too late. Frank had decided he was going to watch the news and there was no dissuading him. Janice could only pray the story wouldn't be on. Let there be some disaster on the other side of the world.

She perched on the arm of the couch beside him, as if she could maybe just jump up and turn it off if the story came on. She knew she couldn't, but she couldn't sit down and pretend to be happy about watching it.

The baby was the second story. Frank shook his head as the footage he had seen earlier was repeated. Then there was more at the end.

"When asked about the dog's history, the police reported the dog was adopted a few weeks ago from the local SPCA. It was a transfer from another state, and they don't have a detailed history of the dog. But they say he was previously owned by a retired couple and was received after the death of his owners."

Janice looked at Frank in horror. She didn't believe for a minute it was one of the Johnsons' dogs, but she knew he would. It was too much of a coincidence. He was already worried about those dogs attacking other people, and now here was something to prove his case.

"No," Frank said softly. He swore under his breath.

"It is not one of those dogs," Janice said firmly, absolutely certain.

"It could be," he countered.

A picture was displayed. Frank stared at it, his face chalk white.

"That's not one of the Johnsons' dogs," Janice told him.

"It is. I remember that dog. He's one of them. He's one of them and he's killed again, just like I told them he would. How could they be so stupid? Of course he's going to kill again. Once they get a taste of human flesh, they never stop, do they? They identify humans as prey now. Not their owners. Not the alpha dog. Food. Prey. And now it killed a baby!"

Janice got up and turned the TV off. He didn't stop her or complain about it.

"We don't know that. It could be a completely different dog," Janice soothed. "It's halfway across the country."

"They said it came from out of state. You heard them."

"Yes, from out of state, but probably just across the state line. Why would anyone ship a dog all the way across the country to be adopted? There's no way it could have come from here."

Frank put his face in his hands, trying to contain his emotions. "How can this be happening? All they had to do was destroy the dogs. Then they would have been safe. How could they not destroy them? So what if people would have complained? People would have been up in arms about innocent dogs being killed, but then at least innocent babies wouldn't be killed! It's all politics! No one was thinking about the risks, the consequences of their stupidity. Just how people would perceive them."

"You have to let it go, Frank. This was not one of those dogs. It wasn't. There are hundreds of dogs across the country that look like that. You can't know it was the same one. Chances are pretty remote, aren't they? The county doesn't have the money to go shipping dogs all the way across the country. Those Johnson dogs would still be local, relatively close. You just think it was one of the Johnson's dogs because you're afraid. It's your worst fear. But it's not true. The Johnsons' dogs only did what they did because they were starving. They were trapped, and there was only one source of food. They're not killers."

"You don't know that. We don't know they're not killers," Frank said adamantly. "And we shouldn't be guessing!"

CHAPTER EIGHT

Sharon awoke in the night as the dogs were moving around, wrestling with the covers.

"Shhh, girls," she reprimanded. "You'll wake Barry up! Lie down! Stay! Or I'll get up and put you in your kennels."

The dogs lay down at her order and Sharon closed her eyes again, shaking her head. The dogs were just too spoiled!

———

When Sharon got up in the morning, Barry was already up. She had a bath and brushed her teeth, and went back to the bedroom to dress. As she was picking up Barry's clothes from the floor, she stopped, frowning, to see what had spilled on the carpet. She turned on the overhead light and put on her glasses and scrutinized it.

"Barry?" she called out. "Are you okay?"

"I'm fine, honey," he responded cheerfully.

Sharon frowned at the stains on the carpet. "Barry? Are the girls okay? There's something on the carpet."

She could hear him shuffling in his slippers to the bottom of the stairs to hear her better.

"What's on the carpet? Did one of them wet?"

"It looks like blood."

"Blood?" he repeated, shock in his voice.

Sharon heard him head for the back door. She put on her own slippers and headed down the stairs to help out.

"Gilda! Goldie! Come, girls!" Barry called urgently.

They must have been playing, because it took a few minutes for him to coax them in the door. As usual, he wiped their feet at the door.

"There's a little blood on their paws," he said, wiping them. "But I don't see any cuts."

He looked all over their bodies, at their butts, and at their mouths. He pushed their lips around.

"Some on their teeth… but I don't see any broken teeth or cuts. The doctor just cleaned them a few weeks ago." He stood up. "Show me this blood. Is it just a few specks?"

Sharon shook her head. She took him back upstairs. He made it up the stairs much faster than usual and stood panting at the top like he'd run a race. He followed her into the bedroom. Sharon pointed to the bloody spots on the floor. Barry cast around, looking for where it had come from. He moved over to the bed and picked up the discarded quilt, and then pulled the bedsheets across the bottom of the bed straight. The sheets were bloody.

"Here," Barry pointed out. "It happened here…"

"They were making noise last night. Do you think one of them bit the other one?"

"They didn't have any bite marks!"

He pulled back the sheet, staring at the blood underneath the sheet, on the bottom sheet stretched tight over the mattress.

"It almost looks like…"

He struggled to look down at his own feet, but his paunch was in the way, and he was wearing slippers.

"Barry?" Sharon said weakly.

"It just looks like…"

He sat down on the quilt box at the end of the bed, slipped his feet out of his slippers and held one foot out in front of him where he could see it. Sharon gave a shriek and grabbed the wall for support. Barry turned his foot this way and that, his brain curiously disconnected from his emotions.

"What happened to my toes?" he asked blankly.

"They ate your toes!" Sharon shrieked. "Oh my—they ate your toes, Barry!"

"But how? I don't… I don't understand!"

"You lie down. You stay there. I'm going to get an ambulance! Don't move!"

Barry tried to bend his knee to lay his ankle across his other knee for a better look, but his old bones and joints would have none of that. He was forced to stare at his toes from a distance, wondering why they didn't hurt. How could the dogs bite his toes and he hadn't even woken up? It looked horrific. He felt sick to his stomach. Barry put his foot back down, into his slipper, and he rested his elbows on his knees and his face in his hands.

"I don't know how this could happen," he said to himself.

Sharon almost seemed to have forgotten him. She was talking on the phone to the emergency operator, running around, unlocking the door for the ambulance, going to see to the dogs. Barry could hear her locking them into their kennels. But they couldn't even have finished their breakfasts yet. They'd be whining in a minute, complaining to be let back out again to eat.

———

At the hospital, Barry lay in bed, waiting for the doctor to come and talk to him and resolve the confusion. Sharon was reading a book in the chair next to him. She couldn't wait anywhere without a book. Barry preferred to watch TV, but there wasn't one available, so he lay there and stewed instead. How could his dogs have hurt him? He loved them and pampered them to excess. They hadn't shown any sign of being vicious. He spoiled them, it was true, but they hadn't had any behavior problems.

Finally, the doctor arrived. He stood at the end of Barry's bed and smiled a greeting.

"How are we feeling then, Mr. Munsch?"

"Well, I feel fine… except my dogs just attacked my feet!"

"It is a bit of a shock, huh?" the doctor asked.

"That's an understatement. I can't understand what happened. They are gentle dogs. They've never acted up."

"Well, I don't think this was a disciplinary problem."

"Really?" Sharon asked. "What happened, then? How could the dogs do this? It's disgusting… It's horrifying!"

"Barry, how well have you been controlling your diabetes?"

Barry looked at his wife sheepishly. She looked grim.

"Not very well," Barry admitted. "My numbers aren't good. It's hard to stay stable."

"Not managing your diabetes can have serious consequences."

"Yes, I know. I've been lucky so far."

"How have your feet been?"

"Until now? Fine."

"Are you sure?"

"Well, yes. I haven't seen anything out of the ordinary."

"How do you explain the fact you didn't feel the dogs biting your toes?"

"Umm… I don't know."

Sharon interposed. "What do you think happened? There was something wrong with his feet?"

"He has ulcers on his feet. I think his toes got gangrenous. I think they were dead. You didn't feel anything because the diabetes is causing numbness in your extremities. You didn't feel the ulcers or the flesh rotting."

Barry felt ill. "My toes were dead?"

"Some of the ulcers on your feet are pretty severe. You didn't notice?"

Barry looked toward his feet, his view blocked by his body.

"I um… Can't see my feet most of the time. Not from this position. Not when I'm standing up. I don't really… look at them."

"And you didn't notice?" the doctor asked Sharon.

"No. He's always wearing slippers or socks and shoes. I don't see him in bare feet. His feet get cold…"

"I see. Well, from now on, you are both going to have to watch fingers and toes for any ulcers or loss of circulation. And we're going to have to get your diabetes under better control. Are you willing to do that?"

"I'll try," Barry agreed soberly. "I knew bad things could happen, but… I guess I just didn't expect them to happen to me."

"It *will* happen to you. All those bad things will happen to you if you don't take care of yourself. So please, do something. Take care of yourself."

"I'll try to help him," Sharon said.

"Good. A doctor cannot be responsible for day-to-day care."

Barry nodded. "What about the dogs?" he asked.

"What?" the doctor asked. "They were taken by animal control. They need to test them."

"But I get them back, right? I need those dogs back."

"I don't think it's a good idea. They may not be vicious, but… you can't take the chance of this happening again. Or of them eating flesh that's not already dead. There is plenty of talk about this kind of thing in the medical community, but there's still not a lot known about the phenomenon. There's no guarantee they won't eat living flesh."

"They wouldn't hurt me."

"I don't think you can be sure. I wouldn't recommend getting them back. And if you get another dog, please kennel it at night. We don't want this to happen again."

Barry shook his head. "I can't just give up my dogs."

"You'll have to. I don't see any other option."

————

After the doctor was gone, Barry motioned Sharon to come closer. He held onto her tightly. Tears escaped his eyes.

"What am I going to do, Sharon?" he asked. "I love those dogs."

"I know, honey. But we can't keep them if they're a danger to you."

"We could kennel them at night. Then nothing would happen."

"You've spoiled them too much. You know how they react when you kennel them. They'd keep you up all night. You wouldn't be able to sleep with them whining and crying."

"It would only be for a few days; then they would get used to it. I can put up with them crying for a few days."

"I still don't trust them," Sharon said, shaking her head. "What if you fall asleep during the day? What if you're watching TV and you just don't notice? Please, Barry. Be sensible. I know how much you love those dogs. But they're going to have to go to someone else. We can't have them in the house where they might be a danger to you. You have to let them go. To be somewhere they would be happy."

"I'll be miserable without them."

"You can get over it. They are just dogs, Barry. I know you don't want to hear that. But it's true. They are not our children. They are still dogs."

"But they're *my* dogs." He sobbed, and wiped at tears. "I love my dogs."

CHAPTER NINE

H i," Frank said. he could hear dogs barking in the background and tried to ignore them and just focus on the person who had answered the phone. "I need to talk to Jim Burton."

"Jim is busy at the moment. Can I help you out?"

"I'm with the police department. I need to follow up on where the Johnson dogs were placed for adoption."

"Oh," her voice was cautious. "Well, yes, you do need Jim. Can I have him give you a call back, officer?"

"Yes. As soon as possible. We may have run into some problems."

"Okay. Can I get your name and number?"

Frank gave his name and phone number, and recited his badge number for good measure, just to impress upon her that it was a matter of urgent business.

"I'll have Jim give you a call back as soon as he can," the receptionist promised.

Frank hung up. He stared at the phone for a few minutes, waiting for it to start ringing, but of course, it didn't. Jim was busy.

The noise of the dogs barking in the background of the call had wound him up. He tried slow breathing to calm his anxious body.

Slow down the breathing. Slow down the heart. Relax the muscles. Recite a mantra.

You are safe.

You are safe.

You are safe.

Frank slipped the phone into his pocket. He took it out, made sure the ringer was on and put it back into his pocket again.

———

About half an hour later Jim Burton called him back. Frank had just started to relax, and the sound of the phone ringing sent his pulse rate through the roof. He took a couple of calming breaths and picked it up.

"Frank Horchuk," he snapped out.

"Uh, yeah. Officer Horchuk. This is Jim Burton from the animal shelter returning your call."

"Thanks for calling me back so quickly, Mr. Burton."

"How can I help you? Stacie said it was something to do with the Johnson dogs."

"Yes. I need to know whether the dogs were adopted locally or whether they were sent to other jurisdictions."

"They were sent to other shelters outside the city. We felt it was better for them to be out of the area, away from any prejudice because of their backgrounds."

"I see." Frank was having problems catching his breath. "I'll need a list of where they all went."

"And this is part of an investigation of… what?"

"It is part of the ongoing investigation into what happened to the Johnsons."

"But that's been settled. I don't understand why you need anything else. I wasn't asked for anything else before."

"Mr. Burton, it would be much easier for all involved if you could just email or fax me the list. Do you have a pen handy? I'll give you my email address."

"Yes—no. I have a pen, but I'm not sending it to you without confirmation. I don't understand why you need it or what it has to do with any current investigation. Why does where they went impact anything?"

"Because we want to do a follow up on them," Frank said sensibly.

"Make sure they've settled in with their new owners. That everything has gone smoothly with the transition."

"So it wouldn't be a problem for you to give me a warrant. Showing I'm allowed to give you confidential information."

"Confidential? How is where the dogs have gone confidential? They don't have any expectation of confidentiality," he teased.

"No," Burton agreed, his voice catching a bit, in a laugh or a sob. "But the people who have adopted them have that right. And we aren't required to turn documents over to the police without a warrant."

"So that's it. You won't give me the information."

"No, sir. I'm sorry. But we try to maintain a proper protocol here. We never reveal adoptive families to anyone. They have a right to privacy."

"Certainly, but…"

"If all you're doing is following up, then it shouldn't matter if it takes you another day to get me a warrant, does it? It's just a matter of following proper procedure. It's just a formality."

"Right," Frank agreed. "Well, I'll be back in touch."

He hung up his phone and stared at it. Not willing it to ring this time, but trying to envision the man who was holding him up on the other end. What kind of stupid bureaucrat would refuse to tell him where the dogs had gone?

Why would they hide this, unless they had a reason to hide it? Maybe they already knew there was a problem.

Maybe they had already connected the death of the baby to one of the Johnson dogs.

Frank just knew there was a connection. An innocent man did not act like Jim Burton was acting.

Shirley watched the dogs carefully as they were trained to attack and release. At first, they were to attack objects or dummies. Then they moved up to people dressed in protective gear so the dogs couldn't actually hurt them. She watched for any sign of too much aggression. Or fear.

Shirley watched their ears and other body language for any sign they were not cut out for this work. It was amazing how much you could read about a dog by watching his ears.

"That's right," she encouraged. "Make sure he's got a good grip, but don't let him wrestle or tear away. Christine, has Bandit got a tight hold?"

Christine examined Bandit's hold on the man's well-padded arm and nodded.

"He's good. Break, Bandit. Break off."

Bandit released the man and sat back on his haunches, smiling a doggie grin and slapping his tail to the ground.

"Oh, you like this, do you?" Shirley asked. "Make sure he doesn't think it's tug of war or a game. This is a job. Attack and break. He has to be willing to do both instantly on command. No hesitation and no play-fulness."

Christine nodded in agreement and continued the training.

———

Frank sat down at the table and picked up the mug of coffee Janice had put down before him. He closed his eyes and took a long swallow. It burned, but he needed it badly.

"Bad night?" Janice asked.

"I feel like I didn't sleep a wink." Frank rubbed his eyes. "All night I just… you know."

Janice shook her head. "I want you to see somebody. You have to get some sleep, or you're not going to be able to perform your job. You look like death."

Frank shook his head. "I'm fine. It was just one night. I'll sleep better tonight because I'll be more tired."

"You'd better put some ice on your eyes because those bags are going to be a huge tip-off."

"They'll look okay after I shower. You worry too much."

"*You're* one to talk."

Frank grinned sheepishly. "Yes, dear."

He picked up the newspaper and tried to focus on the headlines. "Anything in the news today?"

"I haven't looked at it yet. I don't know."

Frank flipped through a few pages. His eyes focused on the word 'dog,' and he tried valiantly to ignore it, but found his eyes drawn back to the article. Just to double check. He scanned the article and then read it more carefully, frowning. He closed the paper slowly, not looking at his wife.

"What is it?" Janice asked.

"Nothing."

"Are you sure?"

Frank shrugged and sipped his coffee again, hoping the caffeine would clear his head. "I'd better go shower," he said. He took the coffee mug with him upstairs.

———

Janice opened the newspaper and looked for what Frank had seen. Her eyes quickly found the dog article. 'Dogs eat owner's toes.' Lovely. Just the thing Frank needed to read after another sleepless night haunted by the Johnsons' dogs.

She read through the article and read about the diabetic man whose cocker spaniels had eaten the dead, decaying flesh off of his rotting toes. She wasn't so sure she wanted breakfast after reading it. It was not an image she wanted to consider. The poor man.

But it was nothing to do with the Johnson dogs. At least Frank hadn't suggested that it did. Maybe that was progress.

It was pure sensationalism. Nobody wanted to read about dogs eating their living owner's toes, but everyone who saw the article would read it, horrified, wanting to understand what had happened.

The shower started upstairs and Janice closed the paper.

———

"Frank, have a seat," Captain Errol invited.

Frank sat down slowly. The captain didn't invite an officer to sit down unless something was very wrong. Updates and orders were given standing up, on the run, in and out. Sitting down meant a real conversation, deep background, maybe a reprimand or disciplinary action. Frank shifted uncomfortably, his stomach tight and his heart thumping quickly.

"How are you feeling, Frank?" the captain asked kindly.

"I'm fine sir."

"I've been thinking about the Johnson case. I know you took some mandatory counseling after the case, but I'm wondering how it is affecting you. Cases like that… nasty business. Lots of opportunity for ongoing mental distress, even PTSD…"

"No, really, it's okay," Frank said quickly.

"Your wife says you're still having problems sleeping. She says you're a bit obsessive about the case."

Frank stared at him. "You've been talking to Janice?"

"I needed to get another viewpoint on how you are doing."

"Another viewpoint? That's an invasion of my privacy!"

"It wasn't an official inquiry, Frank. It's not written down anywhere. Just a friendly call to the wife of one of my officers to see how he's doing."

"My work has been satisfactory," Frank said bullishly.

"I don't think your work has suffered. I hope not. But there are some warning signs you may be a bit off your game. I want us to look at this together and to decide if we need to take some further action. Unless you want to just volunteer for more counseling."

"I don't need it," Frank protested. "Everything is fine."

"How is your sleep?"

"I've never slept well. I still have some nightmares about the dogs. I'm not hiding that. I'm working through it. It doesn't affect my work."

"Unless you're coming to work tired. If you feel foggy or sleepy when you're on duty…"

"I don't. I feel just fine."

"Good. Are you having trouble moving on? Are you having trouble leaving it alone? The case is finished, you know. But maybe you need to talk about it some more; get things off your chest. You can't truly leave something alone until you've finished dealing with it. Do you feel like you still need to talk about the case?"

"Well, yes…" Frank was hesitant. Mostly everyone told him to be quiet about it. He *did* need to talk about it. But not to get closure. Because he didn't feel like it was over. He was still worried about those dogs. About where they were and what they were doing. But maybe he could talk to the captain about it under guise of 'getting closure' and put a bug in his ear. Make him understand it wasn't over. "I would like to talk about it with you, if you don't mind."

"Well," the captain started to backpedal a little, "I meant if you wanted to talk to a counselor about it. I don't know if I…"

"But if I could… I think you would understand my concerns about it better than a counselor would."

The captain looked at his watch. "Well, I guess I have a few minutes…"

"Good." Frank immediately launched into it before the captain could think of any excuses or distractions. "I'm worried about the dogs being adopted. I heard a story on the news the other day about a newly-adopted dog killing a baby. I'm worried they released those dogs to the public when they are still a danger. I want to know where the dogs went and to be sure they aren't going to hurt anyone else."

"Well, that's really not our place."

"I know, but it would help me…"

"We can't interfere in these things, Frank. The case is closed."

"Don't you think it is important to know what they did with those dogs? What if they are dangerous? What if they are vicious?"

"The experts said they weren't. You're worrying about things that aren't going to happen. Things outside our purview."

"I know. But I need to know. I can't let it go without knowing everything is okay. I lay awake nights worrying…" He pressed the mental health envelope, forcing Captain Errol to acknowledge his needs.

"You don't need to worry about what is happening with those dogs."

"How can you know for sure?" Frank persisted.

"I know. They've been taken care of."

"But Captain… you didn't see those dogs. You don't know what was in their eyes. You had to see them to know. They were not just eating because that was the only food there. They were vicious. They were mean. Crazed. I know; I saw them. Those 'experts'—they didn't see them at the scene. They didn't see them where it happened."

"You need to let it go, Frank. You can't keep bothering people with this."

"Bothering people?" Frank echoed, taken aback.

The captain leaned back in his seat arranging his hands thoughtfully.

"I've been getting complaints," he revealed, "about inquiries you've been making."

"Complaints from who?"

"You've been talking to the SPCA. You've been demanding information, saying the investigation is still open."

"I did…" Frank admitted. "I just want to know where the dogs went. I just want to follow up to make sure they are okay, not a danger to their new owners. You saw it on the news, didn't you? About the dog that attacked and killed a baby down south? It was a transfer adoption from outside the state. It came from a retired couple who had died. It's just… it could be one of the Johnson dogs. If they were transferred out of state. If they were all local, then I know I don't have to worry. But if they were sent out of state… I saw the picture of the dog. It looked like one of the dogs that belonged to the Johnsons."

"And like a hundred other dogs across the country."

"I know, that's what Janice said."

"Janice is right. You are seeing connections where there aren't any. There is no great dog conspiracy. There is no cover up. We just need to let it go. The case is closed. They determined the dogs to be safe and they were released for adoption. That's none of our business. The only thing that was our business was discovering and securing the scene and investigating the manner of death. What they do with the dogs is not a police matter. We have no control over it."

"No control, I know. But that doesn't mean we can't investigate if something looks wrong. That's what we do."

Captain Errol fiddled with a pen on his desk. "I can see where you're coming from, Frank. I'll see if I can find anything out, but you have to promise me you won't do any more investigating on your own. You can't keep going back to the SPCA and asking for more information. Okay?"

Frank sighed.

"They're not going to give me any more information anyway."

"Okay. Then we have a deal. You let me check into this, and you try to move past it. And I would like you to attend some group therapy for trauma. See if you can resolve things a little bit better for yourself. Maybe see a doctor and get something to help yourself sleep. Okay?"

Frank nodded reluctantly. "I'll do what I can," he agreed.

"Good. I want you to be well, Frank. You're a good cop. I can't have you being distracted, or foggy, or anything else while you are out there. You're a good cop, and I want it to stay that way."

CHAPTER TEN

On the weekend, they were allowed to take their trainees home for the weekend. They were to take them out in the community to expose them to lots of different people, and to watch for any negative reactions. Any aggression, any fear, startling at loud sounds, or distractibility.

Christine was happy to take Bandit home. She loved the time they spent together during training and she was looking forward to having him for the whole weekend. She put the leash on him as she took him out of the kennel.

"Hey, there, Bandit! You want to go out? You want to go home?"

He nosed at her hand, and Christine scratched his ear.

"Yeah, love you too, Bandit."

She walked him to her car and opened the door for him. Bandit jumped up into the passenger seat and made himself at home. Christine drove home and took him inside. She showed him to his dishes and took him outside, then brought him back inside to play.

He chewed on a knotted rope and Christine tugged on the end of it.

"Is that your rope? What if I want it?" she teased, pulling on it, and moving her end back and forth. "What if I want to play with the rope?"

He growled playfully, pulling back on the rope, showing his teeth. Christine laughed and continued to pull the rope back and forth.

"You like that, huh? Attack the rope! Grab it! Show it who's boss!" she encouraged.

He continued to worry the rope, greatly enjoying the game.

———

"I think getting a dog is a great idea," Janice told Elsie on the phone, glancing over at Frank. "I worry about you living all by yourself. A dog is good protection. And good company too."

"I'm really excited about finding just the right one," Elsie gushed. "You know how I've always loved dogs."

They had owned dogs when Elsie had been growing up. They had been good companions for her. And for Janice when Frank had worked nights and she was on her own. Frank had never approved of dogs in the bed, but Janice felt more secure with a warm body there to take Frank's place. Now she slept alone, while Frank fought his demons and walked the house.

"That sounds great," Frank contributed, speaking on the extension. "I think it will be good for you."

"I can't wait! We're going to have such fun."

"I have to run," Frank said. "I'll catch you later, okay sweetie?"

"Thanks. Love you, Dad."

"You too."

The phone clattered when he hung up. Janice spent another half hour on the phone with their daughter and then went to find Frank.

He was sitting with his elbows on the train table, his face in his hands. But when he heard her coming, he quickly put his hands down to pick up his neglected tools and look busy.

"Are you okay?" Janice asked.

"Sure. Just had a couple of things to take care of, and I thought I would give you girls a chance to chat."

She watched his hands shake as he lifted the tiny tools to work. His hands had always been so steady.

"It's good she's going to get a dog," Janice said.

"Of course." He laid down the tools and looked at her. His face was an unreadable mask. He was so pale lately. "She's always liked dogs."

"It's great you're being supportive of her. But maybe you should talk about your real feelings."

"My real feelings are illogical and overblown. They've got nothing to do with her." He shook his head. "I don't see how talking about it makes anything better. I'm happier when I can just put it behind me. Forget about it."

He picked up his tools again but dropped the screwdriver clumsily and it went spinning across the table, knocking down several innocent bystanders in the process. He swore.

"I wish you would get some help," Janice said. "I really think you could use it."

————

Captain Errol stopped by Frank's desk as he filled out his end-of-shift reports. "I did some inquiring for you," he said casually.

Frank looked at him. "Yes?"

"With the Animal Shelter."

Frank felt a pain in his chest. He swallowed and took a deep breath. "What did you find out?"

"None of the dogs were adopted locally. They were all sent out of state."

"Where to?"

"I don't know any more details. Just that they went out of state."

"So the dog attack, the baby that was killed, it could have been one of them."

"But that's not very likely, is it?" the captain asked. "You can't assume it was."

"Don't you think we should investigate further?"

"It's not our case. Not even our jurisdiction."

"But…"

"The Johnson case is closed. That was our only case. So we can't pursue it any further. I was only making quiet inquiries behind the scenes. It isn't anything official. Just a courtesy."

"Can't you at least ask them what states they went to? Where that one dog went?"

"I would be overstepping my bounds. I'm not comfortable with it."

Frank bowed his head and picked up his pen again as if he was intent on writing out his reports.

"Okay. I understand."

Errol stood there for a moment longer; then moved on again without a word.

Frank rested his forehead on his palm, closing his eyes and shaking his head.

How could no one else want the answers? Why was Frank the only one who was worried about the dogs? The only one who cared what had happened to them and whether they were dangerous?

———

Frank appeared at the SPCA in plain clothes. He didn't introduce himself as a policeman. He tried to act normal, like he was just interested in adopting a dog.

"I was friends with the Johnsons," he explained. "I know their dogs have all been adopted out already… the receptionist told me. But I was wondering about one of them. A retriever. I wondered what happened to it… it was a little skittish, and I was worried it might have gone to a family with children. Do you know? Where did it go?"

"I thought you were interested in adopting a dog?" the man challenged.

"I'd love to have that dog… I would go out of state to collect it… I don't have any kids at home, and my friend, he's a dog trainer, he could help me to settle it down, to make sure it was safe."

"All of the dogs were safe. We had them evaluated."

"I was just worried about this one dog… I heard it went to Louisiana. Is that where it went?"

The man looked at him, frowning. "I'm not comfortable with this conversation. Why do you care where this dog went? We have plenty of dogs here if you want to adopt one. Good dogs. That dog is no longer available."

"It *was* Louisiana, then, was it?"

The man shook his head. "That information is not available. Dog placements are confidential. Are you interested in one of our other dogs?"

"I'm not asking what family it went to. I just wondered if it went to Louisiana."

"I'm going to have to ask you to leave."

Frank shrugged. He left, shaking his head. It was going to take some more work. He couldn't believe everybody was so concerned about keeping this a secret.

Why did they want to protect the dogs?

This was about people, not dogs. This was about people's lives.

Two lives had been lost already. Now a third? He had to know, and he couldn't understand why everyone was so resistant.

He got back in his car, pondering what to do.

———

The private detective nodded as she listened to Frank's instructions.

"That's fine," she said. "Shouldn't be any problem. The only issue is time. How long it will take me to get in, be trusted, and figure out how to access the records. Of course, it may be I won't even need to see the records. I may just be able to pick up details through office gossip."

Frank nodded. "That would be good. That would be quick. We need to find out as soon as we can."

"Like I said, it is just a matter of time. I'll find out as quickly as I can, but it is not going to just be in and out in a few hours. Not likely."

"I just need to know. I have to find out where that dog went. Where they all went. But that one is the first. If those dogs are killing… we have to protect people. We have to find out."

Anya nodded. "I understand. I'll do my best."

"Thank you. I can't get in there myself, obviously. I don't understand why everyone is being so stubborn about it."

"I think *you're* the one being stubborn," she countered. At his look, she smiled. "Not saying it's a bad thing. When you believe a thing, you have to stand up for yourself and be bullheaded enough to get it done. That's what you're doing. You believe in something. You're doing what you think is right. I admire that." She pushed her hair back over her ear. "But you *are* stubborn."

Frank smiled. "I guess I am," he agreed.

Bandit made it through his training. Not with flying colors, but with good reports and what seemed to be a good, solid foundation. He had performed well in classes and seemed to be well socialized out in public. He had passed the various tests he had been put through over the past few weeks to make sure he would attack or break on command; he would not hurt children, and he was able to remain focused on his duty and not be distracted. He would not respond to commands by a stranger to stop, get down, or break. Christine was proud of his progress and was sorry to have to let him go. But it was time for him to graduate to his new police partner, as a full-fledged police dog.

Carmichael was introduced to Bandit, his new partner. He had not had a canine partner before, but he had trained with another dog and was familiar with the procedures. He held out his hand for Bandit to smell and was given the leash. Bandit fell in beside him as if they'd been patrolling together for years.

"Well, Bandit," Carmichael spoke to the dog in his car as they patrolled the streets, watching for any sign of trouble and taking occasional disturbance calls. "How do you like your life as a cop so far?"

Bandit watched him and panted agreeably. When Carmichael didn't speak again, Bandit looked out the other window, watching the scenery wash past.

"In an hour, we can break for lunch. Think we'll have any calls before then?" Carmichael asked.

Bandit made a sort of a rumble in the back of his throat. He had been trained not to bark or whine, but this noise was much quieter; Carmichael couldn't hear it if he wasn't listening closely. And to him, it sounded friendly. A little mumble of an answer from an otherwise taciturn partner.

"Yeah, you're right, I think it's going to be pretty quiet today," Carmichael agreed.

He kept a sharp watch on the street, looking for anything out of the ordinary, any sign of trouble. It was still morning, so predictably there wasn't much gang activity. Gang bangers wouldn't be getting out of bed until sometime in the afternoon.

"All quiet so far," he reported.

There were a few squawks on the radio, but mostly 'be on the lookout for' and 'reported trouble in the area,' and nothing that panned out into a bona fide call.

Carmichael sat back and rolled his shoulders, trying to loosen up sore muscles. He was glad for a car; his patrol area was too large for foot patrol; but he hated the days when he had to sit for too long. Being stiff and then getting out to try to deal with a physical confrontation was not a good idea.

CHAPTER ELEVEN

Frank checked the sign on the door and walked into the classroom. There were a few people there ahead of him milling around, waiting for the instructor or facilitator to come in and take charge.

They all looked like normal, everyday people. No one seemed to be particularly anxious. No more than would be usual for someone going into a new group therapy situation. Nervous smiles and nods, people looking for someone to connect with.

Donuts and coffee were set up on a table at the back of the room with a sign inviting people to help themselves. Frank didn't take any coffee. He had a hard enough time getting to sleep at night and had banned caffeine after noon in the hopes it would help. So far, there had been no noticeable difference. He put a cruller on a small foam plate and glanced around, trying to decide whether to find a seat or to strike up a casual conversation with one of the other attendees.

A woman in her forties with long blond hair hanging loosely around her shoulders raised her voice to greet the group, inviting them all to grab a donut and have a seat. Social time was apparently over.

The chairs were in a circle. Frank wished they were at least in desks instead of just chairs, so he had somewhere to rest his arms and didn't feel so exposed and vulnerable. To begin with, everyone sat at intervals around the circle, leaving empty chairs as buffers between them. But the therapist knew what she was doing and had only put out as many chairs as there were registrants, so the empty buffer chairs quickly filled up until everyone was sitting elbow-to-elbow. There were only two empty seats left in the circle. Late or absent registrants.

"Welcome, everyone! My name is Myrna, and I'm going to be your facilitator tonight. We're going to dive right in with introductions because everyone is going to feel a lot better about sharing once they know their neighbors. I am going to go around the circle, and I want you to give your first name and something about the reason you are here."

Everyone looked around uncomfortably.

"A lot of you will be first responders and won't be able to give details about the incidents that may be triggering your stress response. Or it may be a build-up of trauma over time and no one specific trigger. Feel free just to give us your profession, so we at least have a starting point. If you are here because of childhood abuses, be as general as you like. You don't have to specify what sort of abuse you went through. Maybe once you know the class better, you will feel comfortable sharing more details. But don't feel required. This is day one. Take your time."

Myrna turned to the man sitting on her left and gave him an encouraging smile.

"Why don't we start with you and go clockwise around the circle?"

The man swallowed and nodded. "Brick," he introduced himself. "And I'm…" he cleared his throat. "I'm a firefighter."

"Great," Myrna nodded and motioned to the next person. "Let's just keep going around the circle."

Everyone used as few words as possible. Frank stared at the floor, his face getting warmer as his turn approached. Then it was his turn.

"I'm Frank. I'm a cop."

"Frank," Myrna acknowledged, and everyone turned their eyes to the woman on his left.

Frank blew out his breath in a sigh of relief. That would be the hardest part. The rest of the session would be easier.

"We have a special treat for you," Myrna announced once they had been all the way around the circle. She looked toward the door, where someone was looking in the narrow window, and she gave a nod. The door opened. "K9 Therapy will be joining us today and throughout the next six weeks, to help make your journey a little easier."

Frank watched as volunteers escorted not just one, but six dogs into the small classroom. They were all medium-to-large dogs, various breeds common to service animals. But Frank could barely even see them. Instead, he flashed back to finding the Johnsons. All those eyes and ears pointed toward him. Bloody muzzles. Matted fur. Sharp teeth jutting from their jowls.

Frank got up from his seat. He tried to mutter an explanation but was afraid it was incoherent. He staggered for the door, avoiding the harnessed dogs. He couldn't look them in the eye.

All he could see was their teeth and bloody muzzles.

"Frank? Are you all right?"

He hurried into the hallway, safe from the beasts. He leaned against the wall outside trying to catch his breath.

Myrna followed him out of the room. "What's wrong?" she asked, attempting to put a comforting hand on his shoulder. "Are you allergic? Is something wrong?"

Frank shook his head. "I can't be around dogs."

"These dogs are specially trained to be therapy dogs. They will stay in their harness and with their handler at all times. There's no danger whatsoever to you."

"No. I can't do it."

"Are you afraid of dogs?" she persisted.

He wiped at the sweat dripping from his forehead with the back of his hand. His heart was thudding hard and fast, and he could barely get enough oxygen to stay conscious.

"Dogs are my trigger."

She swore. "Oh, hell! You're kidding me! I'm *so* sorry. In all the time I've been doing this, I've never had anyone who was triggered by dogs. Nervous around them, but not…" She motioned toward Frank. "Not like this. Do you think you could manage to be in the same room with them if you didn't have to have anything to do with them? You and I can do another exercise while the others are working with K9."

"No, I can't." Frank pushed himself away from the wall. "This isn't going to work. I'm sorry."

"We can get you into another group. I can set one up that doesn't deal with dogs…"

Frank walked away, shaking his head. "No. I'm done. I can't do this."

———

Frank worried when he didn't hear from Anya. He kept telling himself he was being paranoid. She was just doing the job. She had warned him it was going to take a while. He had to trust her. When she had something to report, she would call him.

The days dragged by. He tried to throw himself into his work, to forget about the dogs and just wait until she had some news for him. There was nothing else he could do until she had something for him. Investigating on his own had brought no results. Officially, there was nothing he could do.

Finally, Anya called him with news.

"What did you find out?" he asked immediately.

"I'm sorry it took so long. The records are hard to follow. All the dogs are given a number, so I have to go through the files one at a time to find them. And I haven't figured out yet how the number is assigned—they're not sequential, so I can't look for the Johnson dogs sequentially. I have to go through them one at a time when nobody's looking because I don't know the assignment method."

"But you did find them."

"I found the Labrador retriever. That's the one you said was the most important."

"You found him," Frank blew out his breath. "And he didn't go to Louisiana." He knew the answer even before she told him. He felt a letdown, an assurance the dog didn't go to Louisiana. It wasn't the one that had killed the baby. He was relieved.

"Frank…" Anya's voice was gentle, "…he *did* go to Louisiana."

The world stopped. Frank couldn't breathe. "What?" he gasped. "He didn't go to Louisiana, right?"

"He did. He did go to Louisiana. You were right."

"No… we still can't prove that. We still have to connect the dots. We haven't proven it's the same dog. Only that it was a dangerous dog, the same breed, in the same area. We have to connect the dots."

"Yeah. So do you want me to go to Louisiana? Or stay here and try to track the other dogs?"

Frank thought about it. "I'll go to Louisiana," he said. "You're in place. Keep looking. Hopefully, if I can connect this up, the force will be able to investigate and get a list from the animal shelter. If not—and I'm not counting on it—then we're going to need a list of our own to follow up."

———

"You're going to Louisiana?" Janice repeated.

"I need to follow up on a lead."

"For work? You don't have any authority out of state."

"No… a lead I'm following by myself. Louisiana is—"

"Louisiana is where the baby was killed," Janice finished.

Frank shrugged, his face getting hot. "Louisiana is where the Labrador retriever the Johnsons had went. And the dog that killed the baby in Louisiana was a Labrador retriever."

Janice frowned. He could see she was working on the problem. How to tell him he was way off. That this wasn't something he needed to do.

"That's… quite a coincidence," she admitted.

Frank nodded eagerly. "Yes, it is. A big coincidence."

"But not big enough for the police to officially investigate."

"No. Not yet. But I can't just let it go."

"Why is it so important? The dog has been locked up or destroyed now; it can't hurt anyone again."

"But what about the others?"

"What others?"

"The other dogs the Johnsons had!" Frank blurted. How could she not know what other dogs he was talking about? "They were *all* involved. They could all be violent."

"But isn't it more likely," Janice said slowly. "That there was just one dog who was violent, and the rest of them only participated after the Johnsons were dead?"

"How are we supposed to know? And how do we know which ones are violent? Just by waiting to see if they all go off like ticking time bombs? We have to destroy all of them. That is the only way we will know for sure they are not a danger to the public."

Janice shook her head, but Frank understood she wasn't disagreeing, she was just stunned.

"What about work? Are you taking time off?"

Frank nodded. "All taken care of. I've told them I need some personal time to get my head on straight. The captain's been telling me as much anyway. So I gave notice I am going to be away for a bit. They're happy to have me out of the way."

Janice nodded. "Should I come?"

Frank was startled. "No… We don't have much money right now. And you wouldn't be able to sleep in the same room as me. What with the nightmares and all."

"I suppose," Janice agreed.

She obviously hadn't actually wanted to go along, but was concerned about him and whether he would be able to hold things together while he was on his own.

"So when are you going?" she asked.

"Tomorrow. Hopefully, it will only take a day to get confirmation the dog was the same one—or definitely was not. Then we'll know, once and for all."

Janice nodded her agreement. As much as she didn't want to see him go, to have closure on the issue would be a real blessing. He would finally be able to rest without worrying one of those dogs would cause problems.

Frank went to his hotel to check in, and then went straight to the SPCA.

"I'm inquiring about the dog that attacked that baby," Frank told the man in charge.

"Who are you? Reporter?"

"No, cop. But not here. I'm following up on a case back in New York. It might have been the same dog, so I want to find out its history, where it came from."

The man looked him over. "I don't believe you."

Frank pulled out his wallet and took out his shield. He showed it to the dog man.

"Okay," the man said slowly. "So you are a cop from New York State. But what does that have to do with me? I don't have to tell you anything. I've already talked to the cops here. They came right after the baby was killed. I told them everything I know."

"But they didn't follow up with New York, did they?" Frank guessed. "And you didn't follow up with the SPCA in New York. Because nobody really wants to know what the dog's history is."

The man frowned. "Have a seat," he invited.

Frank sat down.

"I'm Bill."

"Frank."

"Why do you care about this? The dog's been put down. It won't cause any more harm. We didn't make any further inquiries because we already had all the information we needed. We already knew the dog didn't have a history of biting. That's all anyone needed to know and we already had the papers to prove it."

"Well… that might not be true."

"It might not be true?" Bill repeated. "They sent me falsified papers?"

"They sent you papers showing what they thought. But they couldn't know for sure whether it was true. The dog did have a history. But there was a lot they didn't know about him, that they were guessing at. They guessed he didn't bite, didn't attack anyone. But it might not be true."

Bill just stared at him.

"There might be others," Frank said.

"Others? What do you mean there might be others?"

Frank sat and thought about it, trying to think of how to explain it. How to tell him without giving him the details. How to make Bill believe this really was serious without him calling anyone else to complain about Frank's inquiries.

"There was a group of dogs," Frank said slowly. "There was an elderly couple that died. But we don't know if the dogs had anything to do with it. If this was one of those dogs, and he has shown he is dangerous… it may mean the others are dangerous too. And they are still out there. If you just confirm the details for me, I can confirm whether these other dogs might be dangerous or not. If they are… maybe we can prevent another tragedy."

Bill considered this, staring up at the ceiling. "It has hit us all really hard," he said. "All of us here at the shelter. To have one of our dogs involved in something like this. When we heard about the baby being killed, we were horrified. Then to have the police come here and say it was one of our dogs… you can't know how that felt for us."

"Imagine how I felt when I heard these dogs had been released for adoption. Animals I had seen, I had looked in their eyes and knew they were dangerous. But everybody just kept telling me to shut up, saying I didn't know what I was talking about. And then when I heard about this baby… I just knew it was one of those dogs. No one would believe me. There are dog attacks all over the world. There was no way it was one of the dogs from my case. No way. Everyone said that. My dogs were completely safe; they could be adopted into families. Perfectly safe." He swallowed a lump.

"She asked about the dog's history," Bill offered. "The mother. She asked whether he would be good with children. She had the baby here with her when she picked the dog out. I told her he would be safe. I told her retrievers were good with kids. I told her…" His voice broke, and he shook his head. "I told her if there was any problem, we had a thirty-day return policy. A return policy! Well, he was returned, all right. To be destroyed. I was glad to do it. That poor woman. She did everything she could to get a safe dog. And we gave her a killer."

"You couldn't have known if New York didn't tell you. Can you please tell me if it was from New York? Please? Can't we prevent this from happening to someone else?"

Bill nodded. "Yes. You're right. It was from New York state."

Frank blew out his breath. He was so relieved. And at the same time, he had a knot in his stomach. There were six more dogs. Six more dogs that might be killers. All those children and adults who might be in danger.

"Can you tell me which town? Do you have the dog's identification number?"

"Yeah… I've got the paperwork. I'll show you."

"Thank you. Oh, thank you, thank you, thank you."

Frank's eyes teared up. He tried to talk past the lump in his throat. He was embarrassed by his show of emotion. But it was such a relief to finally be making progress. To have someone on his side. Bill nodded understandingly.

Bill got up and went to his filing cabinet. He flipped through the files for a moment before pulling one out.

"Here it is," he said.

He told Frank the name of the animal shelter the dog had come from, and Frank nodded.

"That's it," he said. "It has to be one of the Johnson dogs. Do you have the ID number they used?"

Bill read it off to him, and Frank checked it against the one in his notebook. He couldn't believe this was actually happening. Couldn't believe his fears were finally being confirmed.

Everybody had told him no. Everyone had told him he was crazy, paranoid.

They told him he was wrong, but *they* were wrong. He knew those dogs were dangerous. He knew, just like he knew the dog that had killed that baby had been one of them. He had known it, but no one else had believed him.

He reached across Bill's desk to grab a few tissues from the box, wadded them up and dabbed at his eyes and blew his nose.

"That's it. That's proof. Now I have to get someone to listen to me."

"You say there are others?" Bill prompted.

"Yeah. And I don't know where they are. They could be here; they could be anywhere else."

"That's the only one we got from the shelter," Bill reassured him.

"I'd be happier if they were all here. They probably spread them out, just to cover their butts."

"Did they know it was dangerous when they sent it here?" Bill asked.

"They said no," Frank said. "They said an expert declared them to be safe. But I knew they weren't."

"Well, I guess you were right," Bill said. "Now what are we going to do?"

Frank smiled at the 'we.' It was nice to finally have someone on his side.

"Well, I know I have to find where the rest of them are. I don't know what you're going to do."

"I want to help. And I have to tell the local police it was a dangerous dog before Miss Brooks ever got him. She couldn't have known. He was going to hurt someone sooner or later. It wasn't her fault."

"I guess you'd better," Frank agreed.

"Do you want me to call the shelter? Maybe they'll tell me where the other dogs went to."

"You could try, but I don't think they'll tell you. They're already pretty twitchy. They won't tell anyone anything."

"I can try," Bill maintained.

"Why don't we go our separate ways and meet for lunch to swap notes?" Frank suggested.

He needed to get out of there, get out on his own, away from the sounds and smells of dogs and clear his head.

He needed some privacy. Then they could get back together once they knew something else. And then they could get this whole thing straightened out. They could find those other dogs and have them destroyed. Make sure no one else could be hurt or killed by those devils.

———

Captain Errol was not pleased to hear from Frank.

"I thought you were taking a vacation. Some personal time. And here you are investigating on your own? You're not authorized to be making any inquiries!"

"I know. But I had to know, Captain. I couldn't just ignore the stories in the news and pretend I didn't care if this dog came from the Johnsons. And he did. We have proof now."

"Illegal search," the captain said.

"No. I didn't do a search. I talked to the shelter, and they gave me the information voluntarily."

"You didn't have authorization to make those inquiries. You don't have any authority to investigate in Louisiana."

"I know. But you can still use the evidence. It isn't tainted. The dog that killed the Brooks baby came from our animal shelter. It belonged to a retired couple who died. It is the right breed. If you can just get a warrant for the shelter's records, you can confirm one hundred percent that this was one of the Johnson dogs. And if one is dangerous, they may all be dangerous."

"I'm going to have an awfully hard time convincing anyone to give me a warrant based on an illegal investigation you conducted in Louisiana!"

"Then just say I made independent inquiries, you don't have to say I came out here to do it. But we have to find out where those other dogs went."

"You still don't know this was the dog. There could have been two Labrador retrievers from two different homes at around the same time."

"I *know*," Frank maintained.

"You know one hundred percent?" the Captain demanded. "This is still just a guess. Just a coincidence."

"No, it isn't. I *know*. One hundred percent. All you have to do is compare the ID number the shelter gave the dog."

"If you know, that means you've corroborated it was the same number on both ends," Errol said.

Frank didn't answer.

"Have you corroborated it?"

"Not in an official capacity," Frank hedged.

"How—no, don't tell me how. I don't want to be complicit in this. You know. You've seen this dog has the same ID number as the Johnson's dog."

Frank breathed out slowly. "I know," he agreed.

The captain swore angrily. For a few minutes, he said nothing, other than swearing under his breath now and then. Frank wondered if he was fired. Just how mad was Errol?

"So this is real," the man finally said, getting back his power of speech. "This is no longer just crazy old Frank seeing ghost dogs everywhere."

"No," Frank agreed. "Now we know for sure this killer dog was one of the Johnson dogs."

Errol swore again. "You know what kind of trouble this is going to cause?" he asked.

"No… not really. I know it's going to be pretty bad. But think about how much worse it would be if the public discovered we knew this and didn't investigate it. If we just turned a blind eye and said: 'Well, the other dogs must all have been okay.' We can't cover this up. We have to make it right before someone else gets hurt."

"You're right," the captain agreed. "I just don't know how I'm going to do this… man, have you got me in deep doggie doo, Frank."

"Except it's not crap this time," Frank said. "It's blood."

CHAPTER TWELVE

Carmichael heard a shout and looked around for the source. Bandit's ears swiveled around as he located the sound. A woman stood on the sidewalk, blood on her hands and shirt, shrieking. He pulled over and got out to talk to her, and she pointed across the street.

"There! There! It was him!"

Carmichael turned his head to look where she was pointing. A young black man in a hoodie ran down the block and ducked into an alley. Carmichael had Bandit out of the car in an instant, and they were running after him. He made an emergency call on his radio, hoping it was clear enough even with him running. At least they could GPS his car and phone and get back up to him quickly. He put on a burst of speed to try to catch up to the fleeing suspect.

He could just barely keep up. They took another turn down the alley, but Carmichael was losing him. Another minute or two and he was going to lose the suspect.

"Bandit," he ordered. "Take him down!"

He pointed. Bandit leaped ahead of him eagerly, his feet pumping like pistons. Carmichael kept going, following as closely as he could behind. The suspect had jumped a fence and Carmichael climbed over it quickly. He wasn't as young as he used to be. He landed awkwardly and stood there for a moment to catch his breath, knowing Bandit was ahead of him and would delay the suspect until he got there. He started running again, following the sounds of the pursuit. It was only a few seconds before he heard the suspect cry out. He grinned with satisfaction.

"Attaboy, Bandit," he murmured.

The suspect kept shouting, but Carmichael wasn't worried. The dog was well-trained. He would hold the perp and make sure he couldn't get at a weapon until Carmichael could secure him and put him under arrest. Carmichael jogged the rest of the way up to the tangle of bodies and looked down.

"Lay still and I'll call the dog off," he instructed.

"Ahh! He's hurting me!" the man howled. "Get him off, get him off!"

"I'll get him off when you lay still so I can handcuff you."

"Ahhh!"

Carmichael noticed the blood. Bandit was growling, and rather than just holding the man's arm still, was wrestling it back and forth, tearing at it.

"Okay, Bandit. Break!"

Bandit did not.

"Break!" Carmichael commanded. "Good dog. Break, now. Let him go."

Bandit still did not let him go. The suspect was screaming, and there was a growing pool of blood beneath his arm. Carmichael caught Bandit by the collar and pulled him back.

"Come on, boy. Break. Let him go."

Bandit whipped his head around and even though Carmichael let go quickly, Bandit still managed to graze him with his teeth, drawing blood. Carmichael stared at it, confused.

"Bandit. No!"

The dog had already gone back to his first victim. Carmichael tried to kick him out of the way.

"Back, Bandit. Break! Let him go!"

The screams of the man were starting to weaken. He was sobbing, incoherent. Carmichael grabbed Bandit again, hauling him back as hard as he could, ignoring the frenzied dog's slashing jaws. If he got hurt, he got hurt. He had to stop the dog and protect the suspect. Bandit was growling and snapping and slashing at whatever he could reach.

Carmichael tried to attach a leash to the collar, but couldn't work his fingers around the catch while the dog fought back. Kicking Bandit, Carmichael grabbed at the suspect, trying to get a good grip and pull him up.

His hands were slippery with blood. The suspect realized he was trying to help and clung to Carmichael, trying to pull himself to his feet. But that exposed the perp's throat to Bandit, a huge mistake.

A renewed attack, more blood, spurting everywhere, and the suspect was silent and limp in Carmichael's arms.

Carmichael kept kicking Bandit back. His backup found him, but it was too late.

Carmichael stood there, holding onto the victim, kicking at Bandit whenever he approached. Bandit stood back, growling, looking for an opportunity to attack. Carmichael was barely aware of what was going on anymore.

He was in shock.

In shock at the dog attacking, in shock from the bleeding gashes in his arms. The whole thing made no sense at all.

"Secure the dog," ordered Evans, one of the cops who arrived to help.

The officers tried to corner Bandit and keep him contained. No one had come with a loop to catch him with. A few of them tried to keep him there. The others tried to help Carmichael. They took the victim from him and laid him on the ground.

"Are you hurt?" Evans asked, looking at Carmichael's exposed arms and bloodstained clothes. "Oh hell, you sure are. Let's get you sat down, first of all."

Carmichael didn't do anything. Evans gently gripped his arm where it wasn't hurt and pulled him to the side. He found a crate for Carmichael to sit down on. Carmichael sat there, dazed.

"What happened?" Evans asked. "Did the dog just go nuts? Was he hurt or drugged? What happened?"

"I don't know. I don't understand what happened. He just... I couldn't get him to break. I couldn't even pull him off. He just kept attacking. The perp is dead, isn't he?"

Evans nodded. "Looks that way. He's quite a mess."

Evans had gauze in one of his belt pouches, and he carefully wrapped it around Carmichael's arms.

"There. That's the best I can do until we can get you to the hospital. Are you okay?"

"I'm a little… I don't know. I'm a bit foggy."

"I don't know how much blood you've lost. Put your head down."

Carmichael obeyed, but he didn't think it did much good. Evans patted him hesitantly on the back. It was a while before a cop came into the alley who had a loop to catch Bandit. They managed to get it around his neck, and pulled him away, out of the alley. Yellow tape was going up. The forensics guys and homicide were arriving. Chaos reigned in the little corner of the alley.

A few of them asked Carmichael questions, but he had a hard time answering anything.

———

Back at his hotel, Frank tried to distract himself by watching TV. He had talked to Janice, and she was going to bed. He couldn't bear to think of all those families that had gotten killer dogs. He just couldn't bear it.

The news came on. Frank listened to the blather about the weather and politics and other things that didn't matter. It was only on to keep him distracted.

"In the news today, a police dog has killed the suspect in a robbery assault case…" a news anchor announced, and they flashed to the scene. Lots of yellow tape, police everywhere refusing to say anything, and then the police spokesperson talking gravely.

"We are looking into the incident. At this time, we don't have any concrete evidence as to what happened. The dog went rogue… we don't know why. He was a new K-9 but passed his training without any problems, no red flags. We will be investigating further to try and figure out how this could have happened. We cannot comment on the dog's human partner and how he responded or might have been involved in the incident. We will release more information as it becomes available."

Frank stared at the screen. He knew what everyone would say. It wasn't one of the Johnson dogs. Then why were there suddenly so many dog attacks in the news? Was it really just synchronicity? Coincidence? He was seeing it because he was looking for it? It didn't seem like there could have been so many dog attacks in the news before the Johnsons were attacked. He couldn't remember one. And now… every time he turned around, there was another one.

One of the Johnson dogs had been a German shepherd. He remembered it. Remembered the dark blood on its muzzle. Remembered it approaching him with the others, eyes showing the whites, ears laid back against its skull. It was all there, impressed on his memory. It could never be erased. The picture of the dog they were showing on the screen was a German shepherd. But was it a picture of the dog who had attacked the suspect or was it just a stock photo of a police dog from the network's file?

He couldn't call Janice about it. He couldn't even call Errol about it. He had just hung up after talking to him. And the Captain was not a happy man. Finding out Frank's leave of absence had been for more investigating, not healing, had not made a good impression on him. He warned there would be a disciplinary review when Frank returned to the job. *If* he returned to the job. The threat was not exactly veiled.

But Frank could call Bill. Bill couldn't do anything about the police dog, but at least he could understand what Frank was feeling. Frank dialed the number Bill had given him earlier that afternoon.

"Hullo, Bill…? It's Frank."

"Frank? You got something already? That's great!"

"No. Nothing yet. I was just wondering if you were watching the news."

"No," Bill said, not understanding at first. "I'm just getting ready to hit the sack."

"There is another attack on the news."

Bill went quiet. Frank wondered for a moment if the connection had been broken.

"Another attack," Bill repeated. "What happened? Were there children?"

"It was a police dog," Frank told him. "It killed a suspect in a robbery assault."

Bill swore. "It couldn't be another one of your dogs, could it?" he demanded.

"It could be. There was a German shepherd."

"But… the police screen their dogs. They are so careful. Their training is rigorous."

"Well, they missed something, no matter where that dog came from.

I'm telling you, these dogs are vicious. But they're cunning. They don't show their true nature ahead of time. You never saw it in the Brooks' dog, did you?"

"It was a very submissive dog. I wouldn't have been surprised if it nipped someone when it was scared, but to attack a baby… no, I never saw any aggressive signs. He seemed like a fine dog. And retrievers are great for families. Stable. Easygoing. Good with kids."

"Usually," Frank amended.

"Yeah, usually. We know he didn't turn out to be."

Frank shook his head. "What are we going to do? We have to track all these dogs down, and we need to do it now. We can't wait until we hear about each one of them in the news."

"What are the chances they are all vicious?" Bill asked. "I can't imagine every one of them is aggressive. Dogs have different personalities, and even when raised in the same household…"

"These dogs have tasted human blood. You know what they say about that."

"It's an old wive's tale. An urban legend. They aren't any more likely to attack after having tasted human blood."

"Is it? What about the Brooks baby? What about that dog? It attacked without provocation. Just attacked a baby, as if it were prey. It had a taste for human blood."

"So far we only have proof one of the dogs was vicious. Let's not jump ahead just yet. Let's find out where the other dogs went before we assume they're all vicious. This one… this might just be a coincidence."

"Maybe the retriever was the only dog who was vicious out of the bunch." Frank said. "It was, what, the leader of the pack?"

"If the dogs killed the Johnsons—and that's still an if, because we don't know what killed them—that doesn't mean all of them killed them. It could be one of them killed, and the others just happened to be hungry and fed themselves. We don't know they *all* attacked as a pack."

"Dogs hunt in packs, don't they? Not individually?"

"Dogs will hunt individually as well. You've heard of a lone wolf. We don't know the whole pack is vicious. Maybe it was just this one. The one that killed the baby."

Frank breathed out heavily. "I hope you're right, Bill. That would sure make me a lot happier. But right now… I'm just so scared. So scared for all of those families out there, taking home these lovely new dogs to be companions for their children… I just can't imagine what a horror it must be for them. For people like Mrs. Brooks, finding her baby girl, killed, viciously and for no reason."

"The dog had a reason. We just don't know what it was."

"Because the dog had a taste for human blood, and saw the baby as prey. What else could it be? This is not a dog attacking because somebody got too close to its food, or threatened it, or approached it while chained up. This dog went hunting when its owner was out of the way. He had already killed smaller animals."

"I just can't believe it," Bill said. "Maybe something startled it. Maybe the baby cried, and the dog perceived it as a threat. I don't know. I can't believe it just wanted… a snack."

Frank tried to laugh, but it came out as a sob.

"A snack," he repeated. "Just a snack. Heaven help those families. We have to find them, Bill. We just have to."

"We will. As soon as I can find out more information, I'll let you know. We'll contact the families and warn them before anyone else is killed."

CHAPTER THIRTEEN

Come on, Shep," mary Beamer invited. "Come on, boy!"

"Shep?" Alexander asked. "Really?"

Mary grinned. "I like the name! And he's a herding dog, right, so Shep works, right?"

"It's a little cliché," Alexander pointed out.

"Well, where do you think the clichés came from? They're clichés because they work."

"So you say."

"It's going to be so great, having him with the kids." Mary giggled. "He can keep them all rounded up for me."

"Has he been taught to herd?"

"No, it's in his blood. He doesn't need to be taught."

"Well, I think he needs to be taught to do it on command, or to herd them where you want."

Mary shrugged. "We'll cross that bridge when we come to it."

Alexander nodded. He didn't really care. Maybe she would keep the dog, maybe not. Mary went through new ideas and brilliant plans all the time. That's just the way she was. This week's brilliant plan might be next week's disaster, but things were never boring. They went back into the house.

"Well, I'm going to go sort the laundry, unless there's something else you want me to do," Alexander said.

Mary cocked an eyebrow. "You really feel like sorting laundry?"

"I really need a couple of pairs of clean socks this week," he pointed out. "Preferably matched pairs. Things don't go so well when I show up at a presentation or a board meeting without socks. Or with one Scooby Doo and one Barbie."

Mary laughed loudly. "Okay, you go match. I'll work on supper for the crew."

Alexander left her to her pots and pans. When he pulled the warm laundry out of the dryer, he had to fend off two of the children, who wanted to make a big laundry pile and crawl into it to snuggle.

"Not today, guys," he said. "This is my laundry, and I need it now."

"But it's so nice and cuddly," Peeps complained.

"I know it is. So put another load in. There's always lots of laundry to do around here."

Peeps looked to Sarah with a big grin. "Let's do laundry!" she said excitedly.

Sarah's face brightened. "Okay," she agreed. "There's a whole bunch in my room."

They both scampered off to collect a load of laundry, leaving Alexander shaking his head. Would they actually get a load washed and dried, or would they forget about it, instantly distracted by something else they ran across in their room or on the way down to the basement? He lugged his load of laundry up to the master bedroom and dumped it on the unmade bed. There was a yowl and a hiss, and Muffin, a shaggy black cat, slithered out from underneath the blanket and gave him a look of haughty contempt. She stalked off to find another sleeping place.

"Stay away from the girls," Alexander told him. "Or you'll end up dressed like a baby doll."

The cat didn't spare him a glance.

"Well, don't say I didn't warn you," Alexander called after him.

"What?" Nicholas asked, poking his head around the corner and pushing up his thick glasses. "What did you say?"

"I was talking to the cat."

"Oh. What did he say?"

Alexander gazed at the gangly youth. "He said I disturbed his sleep."

"Oh," Nicholas nodded understandingly. "It must be pretty hard to sleep during the day around here. It's too bad he's n-n-nocturnal and can't learn to sleep at night instead when everybody is in bed."

"Well, nearly everybody," Alexander amended.

Nicholas shrugged. He turned to go back into his room.

"Okay," he said absently and disappeared from view. Alexander started to sort and fold the laundry, quickly snatching up the pairs of socks he could spot and tucking them deep into the drawer where the little sock trolls hopefully wouldn't find them. He'd once tried putting them in a box up on a shelf in the closet, but it had only worked for two weeks before the children had discovered them and started to steal them again. That was the trouble with a house full of kids. There was little privacy, and there was always someone after your clothes if they even remotely fit them.

He folded the rest of the clothes, which were less likely to be stolen, and took a breath. Maybe he would have five or ten minutes to relax before Mary called everyone down to dinner. But as if the quiet inhalation had woken her up, the baby started to cry. Alexander pushed open the door to the walk-in closet where the crib was tucked away and gazed down at the youngest Beamer.

"Hello, you," he said pleasantly.

Suzie stopped crying immediately and raised her hands to him, smiling a wide, toothless grin. Alexander picked her up.

"You're looking very bright and sunshiny today," he told her quietly. "You must have had a good sleep, did you?"

She babbled. Alexander adjusted her on his hip and headed downstairs. He walked into the kitchen, warm from the heat of the stove, fragrant with the smells of a soup or stew.

"Oh, did she wake up already?" Mary asked. "Did you manage to get your laundry sorted?"

"I did, actually. And then she sensed I had nothing to do and decided she'd better wake up."

"Mmm-hmmm," Mary agreed. She bent over to kiss Suzie's forehead. "Aren't you the little munchkin," she said, and then straightened. "I still have to finish dinner, so can you entertain her for a bit?"

"I thought maybe I'd give her to the dog and let them entertain each other," he teased.

"Don't even joke about that," Mary said sharply. "Don't make me think about that horrible story about the dog that killed the baby in Louisiana. What a horrible, horrible thing. The littles can't be left alone with Shep under any circumstances. The pound said he was a friendly dog and great with kids, but you can't trust everything they say. Even nice dogs can turn without warning. I'm not taking any chances!"

"I'm sorry. I was just messing around. I didn't even think about that."

"It's okay. Just… just don't make me think about it. I almost changed my mind and didn't get Shep when I heard about it. But we'll be careful… he won't have run of the house while the baby's inside and I'm out. What a crazy thing to happen."

"Yeah," Alexander killed. "It was just bad luck. It's not going to happen again."

"It could."

He nodded and pulled up a chair to sit down. He pointed out the window and talked to Suzie about everything he could see, turning his attention back to his wife occasionally as she wrangled dinner for them. She was pleasantly overweight, too much cooking and not enough sleeping and getting out of the house. Not that she didn't get plenty of exercise chasing children all day long, but it didn't seem to count against the calories she consumed. She was almost always cheerful and upbeat, taking on situations with grace that would have defeated a lesser woman or man. She seemed to always take everything in stride, calm and cool, acting like she enjoyed the whole business of living. He could swear she hadn't aged a day since they had married.

"There's mommy cooking everybody a nice dinner," he pointed out. "Pretty soon you'll actually have teeth, and you'll be able to eat some too."

"Well," Mary amended, "when she gets her belly tube out. Until then, it's just formula."

"Well, there's that," Alexander agreed. "Any word from the doctors when that might be?"

"Nope. They're still just guessing. Might be a month, might be a year. We'll just have to see what her body's able to handle."

Alexander nodded. "Oh well. She's a pretty happy baby. Not like we haven't dealt with feeding tubes before."

"Around here, you'd think that was the normal way to start out life. Well, I think that's got it."

She reached up and grabbed the cord on the dinner bell, giving it a few good pulls. Suzie started to cry again, but Alexander just bounced her and in a moment she had forgotten all about it and chugged to a stop. All the other children started to arrive at the big dinner table. They each grabbed a plate off of the pile on the counter and lined up by Mary while she dished up their dinner from the pots on the stove. Then they took their seats at the table. Alexander watched them come in, keeping a rough count in his head and looking over everyone's faces to assess how they were doing.

"Is that everybody?" he asked. "I think we're short one."

Mary took a quick glance at the faces at the table.

"Sergei," she said immediately. "Peeps, would you go see if he's under his bed?"

Peeps left her plate at the table and ran up the stairs, calling out to Sergei as she went.

"Sergei, the dinner bell went, and if you don't come downstairs right away, you're not going to get any dinner, and then you're going to be hungry when it's bedtime and you haven't had anything to eat…" as she ran out of hearing, her voice faded, but Alexander knew she was probably still chattering.

Hard to believe that for the first two years they'd had her, she'd refused to say a word. But she was better now. So much better. You hardly noticed her differences when she was with a group of children around her age. She acted younger than her immediate peers, but not so noticeable anymore. And around the younger children, she fit right in, hardly any quirks at all.

In half a minute, Peeps was back, pulling Sergei behind her. He didn't look too upset at this treatment. Most of the kids were pretty good-natured about Peeps. She was just too sweet to get mad at.

"You come when you hear the bell," Mary told Sergei sternly. Then she gave him a smothering hug as he brought his plate up to her. "You don't want to go hungry, do you?"

He shook his head quickly and watched her dish the stew up. Then he sat down next to Peeps to eat.

Supper went like it usually did, with a lot of chatter all around, a few messes to be cleaned up, and of course, kids deliberately being gross or bugging their closest siblings. It was sort of an ordered chaos. Near the end of the meal, Mary made her announcement, cutting across the rest of the conversations with her outside voice.

"We got a dog today."

"A dog?"

There were exclamations all around the table, as everyone abandoned their own topics of conversation to find out about this new development. Some of the youngest children immediately jumped up and ran to the porch doors to look out into the back yard.

"Look! There he is!"

"Oh, he's a big dog!"

"He's so pretty!"

"Can I go out and play?"

"Will he fetch?"

"Can I take him for a walk?"

Mary laughed at their overlapping questions and exclamations.

"His name is Shep and he's a border collie."

"He doesn't look like a collie," Meryl disagreed.

"Not a collie like Lassie. A different kind of collie. A border collie."

"A border collie," several of the younger children repeated to each other, with excitement. They all strained to see him in the back yard.

"Everybody sit back down again. After supper is cleaned up, we'll go for a walk to the park, and we'll play with him for half an hour in the park."

"Yay!"

"Can we go now?"

"I'm all done. I'm not hungry."

"Everybody sit back down. Finish your dinner and then wash up."

Several of the children jumped back up immediately to scrape and wash their plates.

"Not without saying excuse me!" Mary's voice rose in warning.

Each of them sat back down again, and one at a time politely asked to be excused. They washed their dishes and watched out the back window again, full of anticipation.

"If you're done with washing and drying and putting away your dishes, then you should go find your shoes and coat," Mary suggested.

She and Alexander each began to move down the rows of children on either side of the table, helping the littles or the less able to finish their dinners and wash up. A couple of the older kids helped, and then sat at the table watching as the last dishes were washed up.

"Are you guys going to come too?" Mary asked.

Nicholas shook his head. "I don't like dogs," he said cautiously.

"You don't like dogs? Have you ever had one?" Mary asked.

"Yes. They poop and pee and chew on all your stuff. And they make a lot of noise." He glanced out the window at the new dog. "And that one's big."

"Are you afraid of dogs?" Mary suggested.

"No… I just don't like them."

"Well, I'd like you to at least meet him. He should meet everyone in our family, so he knows who is part of the flock."

"The flock?" Nicholas repeated doubtfully.

Mary looked at Alexander and laughed at the private joke. "Who is part of our family," she repeated. "At least come out and say hello to him. You don't have to come on the walk if you don't want to."

Nicholas shrugged. "I guess so," he agreed. "But only if he's on a leash. I don't want him jumping on me."

"Deal. You wait inside until I've got him on the leash."

Nicholas nodded. Mary looked at Kyla. "What about you, princess? You don't like dogs either?"

"I'm tired," she said. "I just want to stay home today. I'll go another time. If you keep him."

"If I keep him?" Mary repeated. "Of course I'm going to keep him! I wouldn't have gotten him if I wasn't going to keep him."

Kyla looked at Alexander, raising an eyebrow. He laughed.

Mary looked over the children waiting eagerly. "Dimitri, you need to get a coat on," she prompted.

"I don't want a coat."

"Did I ask if you wanted a coat? Get one on."

He rolled his eyes. One of the older kids pulled one off of a nearby peg and handed it to him. Dimitri put it on.

"Who else? Everyone got shoes on?"

"Peeps has bare feet," someone tattled.

"Peeps, you need to get shoes on. You can't go to the park with bare feet."

Peeps looked down at her feet thoughtfully. "They are people feet," she objected.

"Not bear feet," Mary said, making a growling face and claws with her fingers, "bare feet—naked feet! You need to put something on them. What if Shep or another dog poops in the grass?"

Peeps made a disgusted face and busily looked in the closet for some shoes. She pulled out one rubber boot.

"I can't find the other one!"

The other children helped her look, and eventually, shoes and boots scattered across the entry way, they were all dressed and ready to go. Mary got the stroller ready and left it and the children in the front yard and went around the back to get the dog. She jangled the leash.

"Come here, Shep. Come on, boy! Walkies!"

He jumped up and ran over to her. He cavorted around while she tried to put the leash on him.

"Shep," she said sharply. "Sit!"

He stopped bounding and looked at her.

"Sit!" Mary insisted.

He slowly lowered himself into a seated position.

"Now stay!" she ordered.

This time, he stayed still while she hooked the leash onto the collar.

"That's better. Now shall we go for a walk?"

He whined, thumping his tail happily.

"Okay. Heel."

He heeled reluctantly. When he got out to the front and saw the bustle of children, he left his place at her heel and barked, running toward them. Some of the children cried out and drew back. Others ran forward, ready to play. Mary tugged on the leash, keeping him back from the closest children.

"Whoa there, Shep. Sit."

He settled back onto his haunches, though he looked like he was ready to spring back up again.

"Stay," Mary ordered. He didn't move. "Okay, guys. Let's introduce everyone one at a time. We don't want everyone to move toward him at once, and we don't want to get him too excited or scared. Dimitri, do you want to meet him?"

Dimitri walked up to the dog slowly.

"Good. Hold the back of your hand out to him so he can smell your hand."

Dimitri obeyed. The dog sniffed him with interest.

"Shep, this is Dimitri. See?"

Dimitri patted Shep on the head and looked up at Mary for approval.

"Good job. Okay, you go over to the gate, and we'll let someone else meet him now."

One by one, the children came to meet the dog. Some were scared; some were excited. Shep greeted each one with a doggie grin and a wagging tail. He didn't seem fazed by the ones who were more energetic or moved too fast.

"Okay, now we're going to go for a walk to the park," Mary said. "Everyone ready?"

The children followed excitedly. Some ran ahead, but none went ahead too far, so Mary didn't call them back.

———

At the park, most of the children went to play on the equipment. Bud and some of the others stuck around to play fetch with Shep. Mary helped Bud to throw a Frisbee for Shep, who was quick and eager to catch it and bring it back. Bud threw a few times by himself and then Mary tried getting the children to throw to one another and then to the dog. They had a fun game going, but the children couldn't get much distance on the Frisbee. Mary threw it a couple of times to watch Shep run and let him get some real exercise. But as always, her radar was on, and she noticed Peeps and Dimitri wandering away from the playground hand in hand. She called Shep to her.

"Come here, boy."

The dog raced up to her. Mary pointed to Peeps and Dimitri. "The kids are getting away, Shep, can you bring them back?"

The dog looked at her face, his intelligent eyes sparkling, head cocked slightly like he was asking her a question. Mary pointed again.

"Peeps and Dimitri," she said.

He raced across the field over to Peeps and Dimitri and pranced around them. The children laughed and patted him. Mary watched him nudge them back over toward the playground. She grinned. Alexander owed her an apology on this one. Whether or not he'd been trained to herd, Shep knew what he was doing. Mary played Frisbee with the other children, watching Shep until the kids were back in the playground again, then called him back.

"Good dog! What a good dog, Shep!"

———

Eventually, the children who had been playing with Shep went to the playground and Mary sat down, with Shep lying beside her. She scratched his ears, relaxing and watching the children play.

"Do you run a daycare or something?" a mom sitting nearby asked.

"No, foster and adopted."

The woman goggled at her. "They're all yours?"

Mary nodded serenely.

"Seriously? That's got to be twenty kids!"

"No, only sixteen, and two of them are at home."

"I can't imagine! How can you do it?"

Mary shrugged. "Look at them playing," she said. "They're just kids. We just happen to have a big, diverse family. They all help out. Once you have more than five… It's not that big a deal anymore."

"But they must need you all the time and keep you up at night. And the cleaning…"

"Everybody helps," Mary repeated. "And the house isn't always tidy! You learn to accept a certain amount of chaos."

The woman turned and watched the children, older and younger, playing on the playground equipment. Shep pushed his nose into Mary's lap, begging for more attention. She patted him and scratched his ears. His tail thumped on the ground. After another half hour watching the children, Mary stood up.

"Time to go home, kids. Let's move out."

There were protests from the younger kids, but the older ones encouraged them to finish up and get on their way without any meltdowns, and eventually, everybody got moving toward the house. Mary left Shep off of the leash and watched to see what he would do. He ran around the group of children, moving in and out, getting pats and attention and making sure they were all headed toward the house. Mary smiled, pleased with his abilities.

CHAPTER FOURTEEN

Frank spoke to Anya on the phone. "Have you had any luck?"

"You're going to have to let me know what breeds the others were if you can. I'm having troubles figuring out which dogs were part of that group and which weren't."

"They would all have been taken in the same day, right?" Frank pointed out.

"But they weren't. They were under veterinary care before they came to the shelter. And each one was with the vet for a different length of time. So they trickled in over a period of… I don't know. Maybe a few weeks."

"And there's nothing on their files to indicate which ones came from the Johnsons?"

"No. Their histories have been… fudged… They don't mention the Johnsons. They just say, 'owner died' or 'owned by a retiree' or 'from a rural farm.' I haven't found any files referring to the Johnsons by name, or to the… er… situation."

"And how many dogs from the shelter went out of state?"

"More than seven. So I know it wasn't just the Johnson dogs that went out of state. I need more information."

"I need you to look for a German shepherd. But I don't know dog breeds very well… there was a Rottweiler… a couple of cocker spaniels…

umm, a golden… Don't know if it was a golden lab or golden retriever… what else…" Frank faced the memories head-on instead of trying to shut them out. Tried to picture each face, each muzzle, as clearly as possible. What else had there been? "Another dog… I don't know what kind. Big black and white dog."

"Okay. That will help. I remember seeing a file with two cocker spaniels sent out together. I'll go back and see where they went."

"It's really important to find the German shepherd. See if it went to Chicago."

"I'll try to find it. But remember, I can't get into the files very often, and it's slow work. I can't be seen snooping around."

"I know. I'm working on it from other angles as well. The guy at the animal shelter here, Bill, he said he'd see if he could find anything out."

"Yeah, he's already called, and he's really spooked people. It's not good. All these inquiries just make it hotter for me to work here. People are jumpy. They don't want to keep hearing these dogs might be dangerous. You need to try to tone it down a bit."

Frank thought about his captain trying to get a warrant to look at those records. That wouldn't endear them to the animal shelter either. But if they were successful, it wouldn't matter how the employees felt; they would be obligated to turn them over. He bit his lip. All Frank could do was pray one of the avenues of inquiry would work out so he could find those dogs and have every last one of them destroyed.

———

Frank was surprised to hear back from Anya again so quickly, after all of her warnings about how hard it was for her to get into the files. But maybe the knowledge that they were sure the baby had been killed by one of the Johnson dogs had motivated her.

"I found the cocker spaniels," she said. "I'm sorry, I haven't found the German shepherd yet."

"Okay," Frank said. "Where did they go to?"

"Midwest. I'll email you the address of the shelter. You haven't heard of any dog attacks out there, have you? Tell me we're getting ahead of this thing."

Frank sighed. "No, I haven't heard of any attacks out there yet. I hope we can start tracking these dogs down before they hurt anyone else. I just can't bear to think of more children in danger. It's just so maddening they unleashed these dogs on the public in the first place. They should have known better. It doesn't take a rocket scientist!"

"I know… It's interesting, being in this environment… They are so scared of what the public will think. They couldn't destroy the dogs and have the public on their case for killing dogs not proven to be a danger. And the guy in charge here, the one who had them evaluated… man, he hates putting down any animals. Even the ones who obviously should be. He sends a lot of dogs out for adoption at other shelters. It wasn't just the Johnson dogs. I'm sure a lot of the other shelters just end up putting them down anyway, but Burton, he doesn't want to be the one to do it. To sentence them to death."

"Sounds like he's not quite cut out to be the director of an animal shelter."

"No, I don't think so. He's running scared now. He looks awful. Pale and jumpy. Losing weight. Coming to work unshaven. He's afraid you're right, Frank. He is terrified he sent these dogs out as family-friendly when they were dangerous. He won't listen to what anyone has to say. He won't even talk to your Bill. But now he knows at least one of those dogs was dangerous. I keep expecting him just to disappear one day, to stop coming into work altogether, because he just can't handle it."

"He *should* feel bad," Frank said viciously. "I hope he rots in hell for what he did. If he'd had an ounce of common sense, this would not have happened. If he had any doubts, he should never have gone ahead and sent them out for adoption. What a coward."

"Don't be too hard on him," Anya said gently. "He's human and he made a human mistake. I can't blame him. He loves these animals. But you have to be mercenary in a place like this. You can't care more about the animals than the humans."

"Yeah. Well, keep looking for the others, all right? Especially the German shepherd. If that police dog was one of the Johnson dogs too… Man, maybe it will finally light a fire under the police department and force them to do something."

"Maybe. We'll see."

———

Frank stared at his laptop screen, frowning. He had tapped in the name of the town in Ohio the cocker spaniels had been sent to, along with experimenting with several search strings. And the story that popped up was one he had seen before. He hadn't thought this one was related to the Johnson dogs. It was the story about the dogs who had eaten their owners' dead, rotting, toes. It had disturbed and disgusted him, but he hadn't thought about the Johnson dogs when he read it.

Two cocker spaniels.

Two cocker spaniels had been shipped there from the animal shelter, and two cocker spaniels were involved in the toe-eating incident. It threw him. It wasn't a violent, vicious attack like the baby or the police suspect, but it was weird and disturbing. He thought back to the cockers he had seen at the Johnsons' house. They were not as threatening as the other dogs. They were the smallest of the pack and hung back at the edges. Obviously the lowest in the pack hierarchy. Maybe they hadn't been involved in killing the Johnsons, but they had eaten their dead flesh, and now they had shown their propensity to do it again, even when they weren't starving.

Frank felt sick. How was he ever going to sleep? He was already fighting with nightmares every night, always dreaming about their attack. Their eyes, their bloody muzzles, their laid-back ears, all advancing on him with their teeth bared, barking and growling, closing in for the kill.

Now he would also be thinking about them eating his toes while he slept.

If he could ever get to sleep.

Mary saw the last of the school kids onto their buses and took a breath and a sip of her cold coffee.

"Well, it's just the littles now," she announced to no one in particular. "Now, we need to take the dog for a walk. Who wants to go to the park?"

They were all excited about accompanying her. Mary bundled up Suzie and put her in the stroller, put Sam in next to her, and helped the little ones get their shoes on and done up. Thank goodness for velcro. Once everyone was ready, she went outside to get Shep.

"How are you, Shep?" she asked. "Did you have a good night?"

Shep panted, wagging his tail, waiting for her to unlock the kennel. Mary lifted the latch. As he came out, she clipped the leash to the collar.

"Go for walkies?" she asked.

He barked once, prancing a little.

"All right. Let's go."

She took him back out to the front yard where the children were waiting. They cheered and crowded around Shep, patting him and talking to him, already an accepted part of the family.

"Okay, now everyone needs to give him some space. We're going to take him to the park. Then we can have some time on the playground."

They all headed out, walking with her, ahead and behind. Once at the park, the kids scattered when Shep decided to do his business. "Eww, gross!" Mary shook her head and watched them get on the playground equipment. She picked up after Shep when he was done. She took the leash off of him.

"Okay, Shep, go for a run," she invited, motioning to the large open field.

Shep didn't need to be told twice. He took off running, and for a few minutes, just ran back and forth crazily, like he'd been penned up for weeks. Sam started laughing watching the dog, his giggles ringing out across the park. Mary had to laugh along with him. There was nothing like the laughter of children. Especially Sam's; he was mostly mute and tended to stay in his own little world.

"Isn't he a crazy dog?" she asked Sam. He didn't respond to her, but Suzie burbled happily beside him, giving Mary a huge gummy grin.

There was a flock of birds on the ground at the other side of the field near the pond. Mary watched the dog approach them. Rather than jumping after them immediately, he crept around to one side of them, cutting them off from the water. Then he made himself seen and started to herd them. It was amazing to watch his herding instinct. He was so happy to do it. Mary wondered if he had any experience, actually herding sheep or other animals. Professionally. If it was just instinct and he'd never been trained, then it was just plain amazing.

The waterfowl got more and more excited as he kept them away from the water, gradually moving them further and further inland. Oddly, none of them seemed inclined just to fly over him and land in the water on the other side. They kept waddling around, honking to one another and hissing at the dog and trying to walk back to the water's edge. The dog kept pressing them, forcing them further away. Eventually, some of them started to take off to fly away. Shep jumped into the midst of them, barking his dissatisfaction with this result. And before Mary knew what had happened, several of the birds lay on the ground, dead.

Mary ran over, calling Shep back. "Shep, Shep no! Shep, come here!"

It was too late; she didn't know why she was trying to stop him after all the birds had flown away or were lying on the ground.

She put him on his leash and looked down at the dead birds on the ground.

"Oh, no. Shep, why did you do that? Why would you kill them?" she asked him, pulling him away from his prey when he tried to investigate. "No. No, we don't do that. That's a bad dog!"

He looked at her, confused. His tail wagged back and forth very slowly. She knew he couldn't understand why she was getting after him for instinctive behavior, but she couldn't let him think he'd done a good thing. She had to get it across somehow. Mary took the dog back over to the stroller and tied the leash around the handle.

"Sit," she ordered. "Now stay!"

He sat down and watched her. Mary went back across the field and gingerly picked up the newly slaughtered waterfowl. She was nauseated. It was all she could do not to throw up at the sight. She took them to the garbage can and disposed of them, a lump in her throat. She loved animals and it bothered her to see them hurt or killed.

"Mama?"

Mary turned and saw Fidel had followed her.

"What is it, Fi?"

"Why'd Shep hurt those birds?" he asked, eyes shiny with tears.

"I don't know, Fidel. I think it was a game for him. I don't think he meant to do anything bad."

She was embarrassed to be seen throwing the birds out. At least the park was not full of people. It was still quiet first thing in the morning. Her face burned, and she walked back over to the stroller

"We need to get going, Fidel. Will you tell the others it's time to go home?"

"Okay," Fidel agreed.

CHAPTER FIFTEEN

Meet your new guide dog," Marilyn said, putting the harness handle into Casey's hand.

Casey couldn't help but smile broadly. "Oh, I can't believe I finally have one," she said. She reached down and patted the dog's head, stroking the silky short fur of his ears. "He's beautiful."

Marilyn laughed. "Yes, he is. Very nice-looking dog."

"All that training… I thought the day would never come!"

"Well, now it has. Let's get acquainted and make sure you are suited to each other."

Casey nodded. "I'm sure we will be!"

"Why don't we take the harness off and put it back on to start with?"

Casey had done this before, with the training dogs. She fumbled a bit with the first catch, then got it right and took off the harness.

"There, how's that feel?" Casey asked, giving the dog a good scratch. "What's his name, Marilyn?"

"Oh, I'm sorry. This is Joel, and he's a golden retriever. He was a rescue dog from the pound."

"Poor guy. I'm glad he was rescued. He seems to be very nice."

The dog was greatly enjoying the scratch, wriggling happily under her fingers. When she stopped, he nosed at her fingers, whining for more.

"Hello, Joel. You're a sweet boy, aren't you?" she purred.

"Yes, he is. Why don't you put his harness back on, and we'll put him through the paces?"

Casey nodded. She slowly pulled the harness on over Joel and did it up.

"Okay. Forward."

Joel pulled forward and Casey let him lead.

With Marilyn's watchful assistance, Joel guided Casey back and forth, and then outside and through the neighborhood.

"Oh, this is wonderful," Casey breathed. "It's going to be so nice to walk around without fear of running into anything."

"You bet," Marilyn agreed. "It gives a person a great sense of freedom. You're going to have a great relationship with him."

"Thank you so much!"

———

Frank awoke from a fitful sleep to the ringing of the telephone. He grabbed for it, blinking to try to clear his eyes. It wasn't light out yet. He couldn't see the time on the clock with his sleep blurred eyes and no glasses. He managed to pick the receiver up and hold it to his ear.

"Hullo?" he said hoarsely.

"Frank. Errol. I need you back here."

"Captain—hi. Um, I was going to go out to Ohio. It looks like that's where the cocker spaniels ended up."

The Captain made the connection immediately. "The guy with the toes?"

"The guy *without* the toes," Frank amended.

Errol chuckled at his morbid humor. "Right. Without the toes. Oh man, what a mess. Well, you're going to have to put off your field trip to Ohio. I want you back here ASAP."

"What's happened?"

"I've got the warrant. I assume you would like to be the one to serve it."

Frank drew in his breath. "You've got it?" he repeated.

"I've got it. So how soon can you be back here?"

Frank pulled the clock off of the nightstand and held it in front of his eyes. "I'll pack my bag and head to the airport. I'll grab a seat on the next flight back."

"I'll be waiting."

"Are you still at work?" Frank asked.

"As it turns out, yes. I'm going to stretch out on the couch for a nap now, and I'll see you in the morning. When it's really morning."

"Okay. See you then."

———

Frank was able to make pretty good time. He caught a cab to the police station rather than calling Janice to pick him up. He couldn't believe they were finally going to see the files. They would see where the dogs had gone so they could prevent anyone else from getting hurt. He was cautiously elated. When he walked into the station, Captain Errol was not asleep, but sitting at his desk sipping a mug of coffee. His eyes were red and his face looked worn. He nodded at Frank.

"You made it. You ready to serve that warrant?"

"You bet."

The captain picked up a folded piece of paper from his desk and held it out to him. "There you go. You mind if I tag along?"

Frank was surprised. "No, not at all," he said.

"Great. Let's go."

There wasn't much conversation in the car. Frank wanted to ask his boss all kinds of questions—how he had managed to get the warrant, why he was now so eager to go over there himself. Frank had to just be glad he had been offered the privilege of serving the warrant himself.

The pound wasn't yet open, but there were people there, so Frank and Errol banged on the doors until someone came to see what the problem was.

"Police. We have a warrant," Frank said, holding it up.

The young woman looked at him in shock. "A warrant? For what?"

Frank continued to hold the warrant up. It said what it was for if she bothered to read it.

"For records of where the Johnsons' dogs were transferred to," Frank said flatly.

She looked at him like she didn't understand English. "The Johnson dogs?" she repeated.

"That's right. Let us in, please."

She stepped away from the door, letting them pass, but her face was blank, shocked. Frank looked around and led the way to the office, where he assumed the files were kept. There was a bank of file cabinets along one wall of the cramped space. Frank was surprised to see Anya standing in front of an open drawer. When she heard them approaching, she turned around, closing the drawer behind her.

"Frank!" she said with surprise.

The employee who had let them in the door stood behind them.

"Anya? What are you doing in here?"

"Burton had asked me to get out a file for him," Anya said calmly, displaying a file.

"You shouldn't be in here," the woman said.

"Could you leave us alone here?" the Captain said to the two of them. "Once you show us where the specific files we need are?"

The woman looked measuringly at Anya and then approached the file drawers herself. She pulled open one and started thumbing through them. She frowned, backed up her search, thumbed through some more files, and went back and forth several times. She paused, scowling to herself, and looked again in puzzlement as if the file she was looking for might just have magically shown up.

"Something wrong?" Frank asked.

"I can't seem to find…" she trailed off.

Frank and Anya's eyes met. She turned back around and without a word, started searching through the drawers for another file. It obviously wasn't there. She turned and looked at Frank, panic in her eyes.

"Look for another one," Frank suggested to both women.

They looked at him, at each other, and turned back to the filing system and each started to look for another file. Both came up empty. Frank looked at Errol.

"Where are the files?" Frank demanded.

"Well, they should be right here."

"They're missing," Anya told Frank. "All the files I have found so far… they're missing."

"Show me," Frank said.

Anya motioned him over and she explained which files she was looking for and where they should be. Errol wandered over to the desk and looked over the papers there. Eventually, everyone turned back to him, looking for leadership. Errol shook his head grimly.

"Who has access to these files?"

"Anyone who works here. *Anyone* could just wander in," the woman said, looking at Anya sideways.

"Assemble the employees in another room. I want to talk to them. We'll seal this room."

The woman nodded and went to gather the other employees together. Frank looked sideways at Anya.

"Do you have any idea…?"

"Burton," Anya said, shaking her head. "Burton is the one who was responsible for the records and for sending those dogs out."

Frank nodded. "Is he here?"

"I haven't seen him yet today."

———

Mary mused over the incident in the park as she did laundry and the kids ate lunch. She didn't like the turn of events. She was going to have to keep a close eye on Shep over the next little while. Make sure he didn't get the chance to repeat the savaging of the birds. It was instinct. She understood that. He was an animal, and he didn't understand she didn't want him to kill the birds. But she knew it must be possible to train the behavior out of him. After all, shepherds wouldn't allow an undisciplined dog to kill their sheep. Hunters wouldn't accept a dog who killed their targets. How many times had she heard a retriever described as bringing back the hunters' dead birds without ever breaking the fowl's skin? A working dog would never be allowed to kill.

She'd have to give the shelter a call and see who they knew that would help her to train the dog better.

When she put all the littles down for quiet time, Mary decided to log onto the internet and see what information she could find there about training dogs to herd small animals without harming them.

CHAPTER SIXTEEN

"If that dog is biting, you cannot keep it," Margot insisted to her son.

Scott shook his head. "He's *my* dog," he growled with a sullen, stubborn look that only a teenager could have managed. He swept too-long, black bangs away from his eyes. "Thomas hasn't hurt anyone. People just need to leave him alone."

"He's not safe, Scott. He could turn on you! You don't know."

"I *do* know. It's just because other people bug him or get too close to him. He's never snapped at me."

"He's being way too aggressive. I can't get close to him without him growling and snarling at me. He's nipped or snapped at a couple of people now. We're really lucky he hasn't injured anyone. We'd be in serious trouble and he would have to be put down."

"I don't want to give him away," Scott protested. "Why should I have to when he hasn't hurt anyone? He's my dog."

"But you're living in my house and you're a minor, so I'm responsible for whatever that dog does. And I don't want to be responsible for him injuring someone. You hear about dog attacks in the news all the time. Just think about the story of that baby. It was killed by a dog the owners thought was safe. They weren't watching for the warning signs. But you have to. When you see a dog is being nasty like this, you have to do something about it."

"So why don't I take him for, like, training? Why do I have to get rid of it?"

"I don't trust him, Scott. It doesn't matter how much training he has; I just don't trust him."

"You didn't want me to get a Rottweiler in the first place. This is just your prejudice against the breed."

"No, it's not. I know Rottweilers can be nice dogs. I'm sure pit bulls can be too. But they can also be unpredictable, especially around children, and they are big enough and strong enough to do real damage. If he was a Chihuahua, I wouldn't be nearly as worried about it, because even if it attacks, you're strong enough to defend yourself against it. But a big dog like Thomas? You just can't, Scott. If he went for your throat, it would be too late to do anything for you."

Scott rolled his eyes, shaking his head and crossing his arms over his chest. "So I don't have a choice in the matter."

"No, you don't. I'm the one who would be held legally responsible, so I am the one who has to make the choice. And I say he goes."

"So that's it. You know if you take him back to the pound and tell them he's too aggressive, they'll put him down."

"You're probably right," Margot allowed.

"So can I at least find another home for him myself? Someone who will look after him and not put him down?"

Margot frowned. She thought about it, trying to ignore Scott's belligerent expression. He fully expected her to tell him no. And he was ready to fight over it.

"On two conditions. It has to be someone who has experience with training big dogs, and you have to tell them he has been aggressive."

Scott opened his mouth to argue; then thinking further on it, he shrugged. "Fine," he agreed. "But I'm keeping him until I find someone."

"No. You can keep him for no more than a week. You will need to find someone in that time or he goes to the pound."

"That's not fair!" Scott shouted. "That's not enough time to find someone. Not when you're putting all these conditions on me. Could *you* find him a new home in a week? That's crazy!"

He was probably right. Even giving away a cat for free took more than a week. But she was terrified that Thomas was going to attack her or Scott, or someone else and she wanted him out of her house.

"Okay, two weeks," she agreed. "But he has to be kenneled or on a leash at all times. You can't have him out and just playing around. He has to be under control all the time. And if he growls or snaps at you, he's not allowed out of the kennel until we find a new owner."

"That's not fair! A dog needs exercise—"

"It won't kill him to be in a kennel for a couple of weeks. He has room to walk around in there. But I don't want him out. You can't let him run loose, or take him to the park to play Frisbee. He has to be controlled."

"Fine. Now I know you just want to kill him. You don't care about him at all. Or about me and how it would make me feel!"

"I do care about you. And I care about all living creatures. I'd be much happier to have him go to a trainer who can rehabilitate him. But I don't want to take the chance he is going to hurt anyone. I'd rather he was put down than he hurt you."

"It's not going to happen. He's not vicious. He just doesn't like people in his space. Dogs are territorial."

"Yes, they are. And the kennel is his territory. I don't want him out of there unless he is on a leash. And you keep him on a short leash. Don't take any chances. Just think about how you would feel if you saw him hurt someone. Think about the nightmares you would have. You don't want that."

———

Burton wasn't at the shelter. Nor did he get there. The employees all looked baffled and couldn't fathom where the files could have disappeared to. Frank did a quick canvass of the building, looking for any files that were obviously out of place, checking garbages and anywhere else they might have been stashed. He came up empty. Calls to Burton's home were not bringing any results.

"He's run," Errol speculated. "He heard what was going down and he took off. He's in the wind."

Frank shrugged. "Maybe," he agreed. "Mind if I go over there to check things out?"

Captain Errol shook his head. "We'll send some uni's over. They can check it out just as easily as you could."

The news from the uniformed officers was not good. The super had let the officers into the apartment when there was no answer, and they had discovered Burton's body along with a brief note scrawled on the back of a utility bill.

He told me the dogs were harmless.

"Suicide?" Frank asked in disbelief. "This is not good news."

"No," Errol agreed. "There were ashes from a fire in the fireplace. Doesn't take a forensics expert to tell it was papers rather than wood. Nothing salvageable."

Frank nodded, swallowing. "But the employees… They'll remember where the dogs were sent. That's all we need to know."

Errol shrugged his shoulders.

"There are a lot of places the dogs could have gone, and there are a lot of dogs being trafficked back and forth. It's going to be hard to pin down which dogs were the Johnson dogs without the identification numbers and finding exactly which shelter each of the dogs went to."

And he was right. The employees, when asked, remembered only the most general information. The Rottweiler had gone to Florida, for instance. Where in Florida? There were a hundred shelters he could have gone to. Replicate the problem for each of the dogs… with the records gone, it was going to be hard even to prove the dogs they had tracked down so far were the Johnson dogs.

———

Joel was a good worker, and Casey was delighted with the sense of freedom he brought to her. And of course, everyone loved him and wanted to stop to talk to him and pat him while he was working. Casey took it good-naturedly, putting up with the interruptions and questions and trying to use the opportunity to educate people about blindness and guide dogs. Joel was good about strangers but did sometimes get distracted from his job, or get startled when someone approached him. A couple of times Casey jumped when Joel barked or yipped because a child or passerby had reached out to pat him unexpectedly. She would soothe Joel, and he'd get back on track again.

What struck her as odd was how active he was at night. She supposed being descended from wolves, dogs must have some nocturnal genes, but she had never heard from her friends that their dogs were so active at night. He worked so hard all day; she would have thought he would be too tired to be up at night. But Casey often awoke to strange noises or sudden crashes as Joel roamed the apartment and got into things.

When she talked to Marilyn about it, Marilyn's voice was puzzled.

"No, he shouldn't be doing that. You should kennel him at night so he'll be quiet and won't get into things, and so he has enough energy to work during the day. I've never heard of a guide dog behaving that way before."

"Huh." Casey shrugged. "I guess he's just a night owl. I'll try kenneling him and see if he'll stay quiet then."

But that didn't go over well. He howled when he was caged and wanted to be out. She tried putting a blanket over the kennel, but it didn't help. He just chewed it to bits and still howled and pranced around the cage like he was looking for a way out. The neighbors were complaining, and the landlord said that even though Joel was a guide dog, if he didn't shut up, the man would have to evict Casey.

So she eventually gave up and went back to letting him roam at night.

CHAPTER SEVENTEEN

So you're Scott?" the man asked.

Scott nodded and put his hand out to shake like a grown up. The man hesitated for a minute and then put out his hand and shook Scott's firmly. He was a small, slight man, with a shaved head and tattoos. He had a five o'clock shadow, and it was still morning. He looked tough and angry.

"I'm Miles," he said.

"Great. So, you're interested in my dog?"

Miles shrugged. "Why don't you tell me about him? He's a Rottweiler?"

"Yeah. What do you want to know?"

"How long have you had him?"

Scott looked down. "Just for a few weeks. Not long. I got him from the pound. But my mom doesn't like rotties."

"Why'd she let you get him, then?"

"I don't know. I guess she didn't think about it. But she doesn't like having him around."

"What's he like? What's his personality?"

"He's… a bit aggressive. I think he just needs some training."

The man looked Scott over thoughtfully. "What do you not want to tell me?"

Scott stared down at the asphalt. He kicked at a rock. "You probably don't want Thomas," he said.

"Why not?"

"He growls a lot. He's snapped at or nipped a couple of people. Mom says he's too aggressive to keep. But I can't take him back to the pound; they would just destroy him."

"You're right. Pound doesn't like aggressive dogs. And they don't have time to train them. They have too many animals to worry about one dog that doesn't quite have the personality they want."

Scott nodded miserably. "But I want to find him another home. So he doesn't have to be put down."

"Your mom is right too. You don't want a dog like that in your family."

Scott felt his eyes burning. His dog might be aggressive, but Scott loved him anyway, and the thought of having to put him down made him feel sick.

"But an aggressive dog can be okay in other places," Miles said. "If you want a guard dog, you want a dog that's territorial and shows his teeth if a stranger gets too close. You don't want him in a family, but in a place like that..."

Scott searched Miles' face. "Is that why you want him? Are you looking for a guard dog? Because he'd be a really good guard dog."

"Yeah? So can I meet him?"

Scott nodded. "Yeah, sure," he agreed. "Come on; I'll take you to the house."

Miles walked with him back to the house and Scott took him into the backyard to the kennel. Thomas ran up to the chain link of the kennel alertly. When he saw Miles, he started to growl. He lowered his ears and bared his teeth in an ugly snarl, moving right up against the fence. Miles stepped toward him, and Thomas started to bark loudly, jumping up against the fence and snarling, trying to reach him. Miles ran his hand down the links of the fence to tease him, and Thomas went wild. He barked hysterically, frothing at the mouth.

"Stop it," Scott begged. "Just leave him alone. If my mom hears him barking like that..."

Miles laughed. "You're right," he said. "This isn't the kind of dog you want in a family. But I can use him. Whether I train him for somebody else or keep him myself, he's got the kind of temperament I need for a guard dog. Would you go into a yard with a dog like that in it? A dog that wasn't yours?"

Scott shook his head, looking at the dog with new eyes. He'd never seen Thomas as angry and excited. He had always been careful not to upset the dog. But Thomas looked like a dog from hell. There was a wild, crazy gleam in his eye. Scott would never take him out of the kennel looking like that. For the first time, he could see what his mother was talking about when she said he was dangerous. He was scary. Scott swallowed.

"So do you want him?"

"Sure do. How much are you asking for?"

"Just what it cost me at the pound. Two hundred and fifty dollars."

"Deal."

They shook on it.

———

Miles had to spend some time standing around Scott's back yard, waiting for the dog to settle back down again. Then Scott took him out carefully, snapping the leash onto his collar, and without a word, handed the leash across to Miles. His eyes glistened with tears, but he kept his face stony.

"He'll be okay," Miles assured him. "Don't you worry. I'll take good care of him."

Scott nodded. "Thanks," he croaked.

Miles ordered the dog to heel and left Scott's house. He took the dog to his truck and put him in the box of the pick-up.

Miles drove out to his own house, beyond the edge of town. The other dogs barked at the approach of the truck, but when he yelled at them to shut up, they were immediately silent. Miles told Thomas to come and took him out of the bed of the truck and back to the yard.

"There's your new home," Miles told him. "This is where you're going to live from now on. You do what you're told and you'll be just fine here."

The dog looked at him warily. Miles tied him to the fence and left him there. Several times during the day, he looked out into the yard to take a look at the new dog. He was larger than Miles' other dogs. Miles could see he had real potential. When Miles was done with him, he was going to be a great dog.

By the end of the day, the dog was lying down, nose between his paws. When Miles entered the yard, he jumped to his feet.

"We're going to have to come up with another name," Miles said aloud. "Aren't we? How about… Slash? That would be a good name. Do you like that, Slash?"

The dog was studying him; wary and wondering what Miles was all about.

"Sit, Slash."

The dog lowered his hindquarters to the ground.

"Stay," Miles ordered. "Guard."

He went over to the other dogs and checked their water. Then he got out the dog food and approached their dishes.

"You guys hungry?" he asked.

The dogs all sat absolutely still, ears pointed forward, watching him intently. Miles filled each of the bowls and turned and looked at them. They were all still frozen, waiting for him. Miles moved away from the dishes.

"Now," he said.

They all approached their dishes, watching him, and began to eat, one eye remaining on him. Miles nodded. He walked back into the house without looking at Slash or offering him any food or water.

———

By morning, he figured Slash would be getting pretty dry. He went out to the yard and fed and watered the other dogs as usual. Slash watched him. Miles went up to him after the other dogs were fed and looked him over.

"I told you to stay, and you moved," he reprimanded. "That's not good. You need to be trained better."

Looking at him, Slash whined slightly in the back of his throat.

"Nope, no whining. You only do what I tell you to."

Slash watched him with bright, intelligent eyes.

"You want some water?" Miles asked.

The dog didn't react. Miles put a bowl of water a few feet away from

Slash. The dog immediately moved toward it, and Miles kicked him in the nose.

"No! Stay!" he shouted.

Slash yelped and jumped back. He tried to circle Miles but was restricted by his rope. Miles stood between him and the water.

"Sit," he ordered.

The dog didn't want to. He wanted water. But eventually, he sat back on his haunches, eyes moving from Miles to the water and back again.

"Stay," Miles ordered.

Ears pointing forward, Slash sat, watching the water, waiting. Miles moved so he was no longer between the dog and the dish.

"Stay," he said again.

The dog shifted up an inch, then settled back down again. Miles walked to the door of the house and looked back. Slash watched him. Miles went into the house. He looked back out the window and saw the dog at the water dish, lapping it up thirstily. He swore and picked up a length of garden hose on his way back out the door to where Slash was drinking.

"No!" he shouted, bringing the hose down as hard as he could across the dog's body. "No, I told you to stay!"

The dog yelped and screeched with pain and jumped back. He took up an aggressive stance, facing off against Miles, darting out of the way with his eyes on the hose.

"Sit!" Miles ordered yet again.

The dog didn't immediately sit down, and Miles whipped the hose down again. Slash tried to dart out of the way, but Miles kept bringing the hose down over and over again. A couple of times, the dog yelped, once he growled, but eventually, he was silent. Miles whipped him a few more times for good measure.

"Sit!" he ordered.

The dog sat. Miles stared at him, meeting his eyes aggressively.

"You think you're alpha dog around here?" he asked. "Because you're not. I'm top dog around here, and you don't do anything unless I tell you to."

Slash didn't move. Miles picked up the water dish and put it directly in front of Slash. Slash bent his head down to drink.

"No!" Miles shouted, bringing down the hose again. "You don't eat until I say so," Miles warned. He pushed the water dish closer with his toe. Slash looked at it and didn't move.

"Good boy," Miles approved. "That's right."

Neither one of them moved for a few minutes. Miles walked back to the house. When he looked back, Slash was still sitting there staring at the water dish. Miles went inside and looked out the window. Slash was still not moving. Miles left him be. An hour later he looked out again. The dog was still sitting, waiting. Miles went back out to the yard.

"Good boy," he murmured. "Good staying. Now drink."

Slash stared up at him, trying to understand.

"Now drink," Miles repeated. He bent over and pressed Slash's head toward the bowl. "Now."

Slash resisted until his muzzle was touching the surface of the water, then he started drinking. Miles stood over him, watching. The dog's sides quivered as he drank. He had dried black blood in his fur from his whipping. He drank until the bowl was licked dry. Then he sat back and looked at Miles.

"You hungry?" Miles asked.

The dog looked at him, ears back in fear or submission. Miles put some food in a dish and put it down on the ground. Slash looked at it and back up at Miles again. He didn't move.

"Good boy," Miles approved. "You stay."

It had been more than twenty-four hours since the dog had last eaten. But he would learn to do nothing without Miles telling him to. He wouldn't eat or drink anything anyone else gave him. Miles walked back into the house, leaving him looking down at his dish.

———

Casey showered, dressed, and prepared her morning cup of coffee before venturing to the back of her condo and opening the sliding door to the tiny back yard.

"Joel, come on in," she invited.

Last night, he had been making so much noise she had finally stumbled out of bed and ordered him outside. Luckily, he didn't howl in the yard, and she got what felt like the first good night's sleep in weeks. It was as bad as having a new baby. He woke her up with his antics several times a night.

Joel was growling and snuffling something at the far end of the yard and didn't come. Casey shook her head.

"Joel. Come!" she ordered impatiently.

He still didn't come.

"Joel, if you make me come out there, so help me you're going right to the pound! I've had enough of your nonsense."

He sneezed and still didn't come. Casey was getting really irritated.

"Joel! Now!"

Finally, she slipped on her outdoor shoes, stepping on the heels and wearing them as slippers like her mom always used to chide her for. She padded over to where Joel was busy.

"Joel, you little monster, I said it's time to come in."

She bumped up against his side and reached for his collar. Joel barked and snapped at her, making her jump and pull back, shocked. But Casey wasn't going to let him intimidate her. She was not a poor little blind girl who couldn't even manage her own dog. She wasn't going to be calling Marilyn or anyone else to deal with the dog; she would do it herself. She kicked him in the hindquarters.

"No, Joel! Sit!"

He sat down and Casey reached again for the collar and pulled him back from what had interested him so much. He resisted, but she got him back a foot or two and then reached out to see what he'd been playing with. Her fingertips touched something warm and damp, a familiar coppery smell reaching her nostrils.

Casey's throat constricted. "What the...?"

She let go of his collar without meaning to. It slipped out of her grasp, and she heard one last snarl from Joel before feeling his weight hit her body, his center of gravity too high for her to stay on her feet.

———

In the morning, Miles slept in, checked his email, had a leisurely coffee and frozen waffle before going to check on the dogs. He fed his trained dogs first, and they gobbled their food eagerly once given the command. Then Miles went over to Slash. The dog lay on his side, panting, his eyes dull. He didn't look well. He raised his head when Miles approached, his lips drawing back away from his teeth slightly in a half-hearted snarl. Miles laughed at him.

"Get up, Slash. Sit. Up."

The dog struggled to its feet and sat up. Miles filled the water bowl and placed it in front of Slash. The dog looked at it, and at Miles, and didn't move.

"That's right. Good dog."

The full bowl of kibble was still there. Slash hadn't touched it. Miles waited, meeting the dog's eyes, enforcing his position as alpha in the pack. Slash dropped his eyes.

"Okay, Slash, eat and drink," Miles said.

Slash looked at him, ears pricking up.

"Now. Eat."

Slash didn't move until Miles put his hand on the dog's head and pressed him down. Then Slash dove into the food dish, gobbling down the food as fast as he could, his eyes straining up toward Miles to make sure it was allowed. Miles nodded.

"Good dog," he reassured. "You go ahead and eat. You're doing good."

Slash looked away and paid full attention to his food.

Now that Slash understood he could not eat or drink without permission from Miles, it was time to take his training further. Miles kept Slash tied up. He invited some friends to come over to the house.

When they arrived, the other dogs went wild, barking and snarling and growling. It wasn't long before Slash joined them, excited, working himself into a frenzy. The visitors stopped at the gate and waited.

"Hey Miles, man, are you going to let us in?" Decker yelled.

Miles came out of the house. He told the dogs to shut up. Instantly, the older dogs fell silent. Slash kept barking.

"I said shut up!" Miles raged at him. "So you'd better shut up!"

He had a chain this time and began to whip Slash mercilessly. The dog yelped and cringed and moved away, trying to avoid the blows.

"No whining," Miles told him. "Shut up!"

The high-pitched whining stopped and Slash cowered before Miles, pleading with his eyes, but not making a sound.

"That's better. Good dog," Miles praised. "Good Slash, being quiet."

Then he went over to the gate and opened it for his visitors.

"Man, Miles," Decker complained. "Took you long enough."

"I've got to train up the new dog. You don't mind waiting."

"Well…"

Miles swung the bloody chain at his side. "You going to argue with me, Decker?" he asked, with mock threat in his voice.

Decker laughed. "After seeing that?" he asked. "Not me." He looked ruefully at the chain and then over his shoulder at the dog.

"You hurt him bad," Stefan pointed out.

Miles raised his eyes. "Do you doubt my ability to train this dog properly?" he asked.

"No… but I can't say I approve of your method."

Miles shrugged. "I don't care what you think of my method. It's effective. You won't find anyone who can train a dog faster."

Stefan nodded. "That might be true. But I can't help thinking—"

"Don't think, Stefan. You're not here to think."

Stefan rolled his eyes and shook his head. "You got some plans for today?" he asked, changing the subject. "What did you have in mind?"

"Come inside, and I'll tell you what I'm thinking," Miles agreed.

CHAPTER EIGHTEEN

Casey awoke in a fog.

Something was wrong, but she wasn't sure what. She knew she was in her yard. Something bad had happened. Why was she lying on the ground? She got to her knees but was unable to push herself to her feet. She crawled across the ground, eventually arriving at the fence. She followed the fence to the house, found the door, and slid it open. Casey entered the house and shut the door behind her. She just knelt there on the floor for a while, catching her breath and trying to remember what had happened. Was it the middle of the night? She had put Joel out in the yard. But the warmth of the glass in the sliding door suggested it was daytime. Midday, even.

She had put her cup of coffee down somewhere… Casey used the counter to pull herself to her feet and felt for the coffee cup. It was still barely warm, but she felt like maybe the coffee would help calm her shakes.

She must be sick. Did she have the flu? She should call into work and let them know. Casey tried to take a drink of the coffee and spilled it down her front. She couldn't feel her lips or mouth. After trying a couple more times with the same results, Casey sank to the floor again and closed her eyes.

Time passed.

She wasn't sure whether she stayed conscious or not.

She realized she needed help. Whatever was wrong with her, she needed someone to take her to the doctor. Or at least to help her up to her bed.

Casey dragged out her cell phone and punched in Sylvia's number. It rang a few times, and then, to Casey's relief, Sylvia picked up.

"Hi Casey!" she sang out. "How's it going?"

"I need help," Casey said, but the words came out all in a slur. She couldn't seem to form the words. It was like she'd been to the dentist and her mouth was frozen or stuffed with cotton.

"Casey? Is that you?" Sylvia asked doubtfully.

"Uh-huh."

"Are you okay?"

"No—" the word was mush. "Uh-uh," Casey amended.

"Where are you? Are you at home?"

"Uh-huh."

"I'll be right over, Casey. Sit tight. I'll be right there."

Casey put down the phone and waited.

————

Miles went to check on the new dog. Slash lay on his side in the dirt and didn't get up at Miles' approach. His eyes were open and his eyes rolled to watch Miles approach and lean over him. Miles waved away the flies buzzing over Slash's open wounds.

"You gotta learn to listen to me, Slash. You gotta show me respect, or you're gonna get hurt. I'm top dog around here."

Slash just watched him, not moving. Miles filled his food and water dishes and set them before the dog.

"Now. Eat."

Slash lifted his head for a moment, then laid it back down again. Miles slid his hand under the big dog and rolled him onto his belly. He brought the water dish closer and lifted Slash's head, putting his muzzle into the water. Slash lapped at it weakly. After a few moments, he lifted his head up a bit on his own and shifted his body into a more upright position, though he still didn't stand. When he stopped drinking, Miles switched bowls, putting the food dish under Slash's nose.

"Eat," he said. "It's okay. Now. Eat."

Slash took a few bits of kibble at a time, chewing on them briefly, and then swallowing them.

"That's right," Miles said. "Good boy."

He was relieved the dog was not too weak to eat. He'd been worried at first Slash didn't have the spirit to keep going. He'd paid good money for the dog, and he would hate to lose him because he was too weak to survive training.

When Slash was finished eating and put down his head, Miles picked him up and moved him a few feet away, so he could wash away the blood on the pavement.

———

The dogs were going crazy. Miles walked to the window and looked out. A white van was at the entrance to his property. He swore. It did not look good. He walked out of the house and up to the fence. The sign on the side of the truck said 'bylaw enforcement.' Miles spit to the side. Not good at all.

"What do you want?" he demanded.

"We've had a complaint about your dogs," the uniformed bylaw officer told him.

"Shut up!" Miles yelled at the dogs and the noise shut off like a tap. He favored the bylaw enforcement officer with a glare.

"What's your name?"

"Evans."

"Well, Mr. Evans, my dogs have not been bothering anyone. I'm too far away for anyone to worry about the noise, and as you can hear, they stop when I tell them to. The only time they bark is when there is an intruder around my yard. They're guard dogs. That's what they're supposed to do. And they haven't been at large or bitten anyone. So what's the problem?"

"Will you let me in, please?"

"Like hell! You've got no right to come onto my property."

"I am authorized by the municipality—"

"You're not authorized by me. So you can just stay where you are."

"I need to see the dogs."

"Nope."

"If I have to call the police to get access to your dogs, you will be placed under arrest."

"So what? I'm not going to prison for refusing to let bylaw onto my property. At most, I'll get a stern warning and a fine. You just stay away from my property. Tell your boss you checked it out and everything looked fine. I don't cotton to wannabe cops on my property."

"I can't do that, Sir. This is your last warning. Let me in, or I'll have the police come and force the locks and arrest you. I need to see those dogs."

Miles swore and shook his head, but he unlocked the gate to let Evans in.

Evans nodded. "Thank you," he said politely.

He walked over to look at the dogs. Miles went back into the house. A while later, Miles watched through the window as Evans caught the dogs with neck loops and transferred them to the van, and then picked up Slash and put him in the van. He left a pink summons stuck to Miles' door and drove away.

———

"Oh no," Frank said aloud, as the TV reporter turned to the next story—an autistic boy who had been savaged by his pet dog. Frank reached for the phone, watching the screen.

"You often hear about how good dogs are for autistic children," the reporter started. "And there are dogs specially trained as service dogs for those who need them. But as a California foster mom recently found out, not all dogs are good for all autistic kids. Mary Beamer adopted a border collie from the local SPCA, hoping he would help out with her children, both foster and adopted. She currently has sixteen of them! One is fourteen-year-old Nicholas, a high functioning autistic boy who had been passed from home to home until he finally found the Beamers and found his place there. He has flourished under their care, gaining in confidence, becoming mainstreamed at school, and learning skills through various programs. Everything was going great for him, until this afternoon…"

Frank missed the next few details as Errol answered his phone.

"Turn to the six o'clock news," Frank said

"What?" Errol swore under his breath. Frank heard him flipping on the TV, then heard the same feed over the receiver as he was watching on the TV.

"At first, things seemed to be going great between Shep and the children. Being a herding dog, he worked well with the children when they went on outings. But Nicholas was afraid of dogs and preferred to watch Shep from a distance. Witnesses say Nicholas had wandered from the playground where the other children were playing, and when Shep went to round him up, Nicholas ran away. The dog pursued, and when he caught up with the boy, attacked him. Nicholas is in stable condition in the hospital, with injuries to his legs, back, arms, and face."

As they moved into the next story, Frank muted the TV. Errol did the same. They were both silent for a moment.

"One of ours?" Errol asked.

"Our border collie went to California."

Errol swore fiercely. "Are we ever going to get ahead of this thing?" he demanded. "It doesn't seem to matter how much manpower we put on tracking these dogs down; we can't get ahead of them. How could they all be violent? It doesn't make sense, Frank. How could all of them be vicious? I could understand one or even two, but to have all of them show up in the news like this… It's creepy."

Frank suppressed a shudder. "Do you still believe they just happened to feed on the flesh of their owners who just happened to die of natural causes?" he asked.

"Hell, no!" the captain responded vehemently. "Those dogs attacked and killed the Johnsons. Nothing else makes sense."

"Yeah," Frank agreed.

He closed his eyes and breathed for a moment, trying to move past the images of the dogs barking and snarling at him.

He needed to stay focused on the present, figure out how to solve this thing. With the support of the police department behind him, it had to be easier. But most of the dogs had gone to rural areas, small shelters not even on the internet. Some of them not even in the phone listing. And the little rural shelters hardly kept any records. A receipt with a credit card number on it, no tracking of the individual dogs; they operated like a street-corner lemonade stand.

"We'll find them," Errol promised. "Somehow."

"I'm just afraid the only way we're going to find them is hearing about them on TV," Frank sighed. "So far out of seven, we have five—the lab, the German shepherd, the two cockers, and now the border collie. We are still missing the Rottweiler and the golden retriever."

"The Rottweiler went to Florida."

"I heard." Frank's stomach clenched. "That's where my daughter is. I haven't been able to get a hold of her. Believe it or not… she recently adopted a new dog."

Errol's voice was cautious. "What breed?"

"I don't know." Frank swallowed. "I never asked."

"I'm sure she's all right. Just because we're dealing with this situation… that doesn't mean everyone who adopted a dog is in danger. There are only two more out there."

"And one of them is the Rottweiler," Frank said, trying to shrug off his goosebumps. "That Rottweiler was a devil. I remember the look in his eye."

"We'll find him. We'll have him by tomorrow," Captain Errol promised.

Frank looked down, nodding. "Absolutely," he agreed. "By tomorrow."

———

When Frank still hadn't heard back from Elsie by the next morning, Janice was getting concerned too. She still wasn't worried about the dog, but she wondered what had happened. Elsie had always been responsible. She'd always kept in contact with them, returned their calls promptly, and done all the right things. It didn't make sense for her not to call back. Something was wrong. Frank made a decision.

"I'm flying out there."

"Frank, you can't," Janice protested weakly. "Your job… the money…"

"It doesn't matter. I have to find Elsie, make sure she's okay. Everything else is secondary."

"I'm sure we're just overreacting."

"No. We're not. She hasn't answered her phone in twenty-four hours. Something is wrong."

"There's probably a perfectly reasonable explanation," Frank agreed. "But… I have to go. I have to make sure. What do we know about this dog she adopted? Anything?"

Janice was reluctant to answer. "Not very much," she admitted. "But it isn't one of the Johnson dogs. She said it was taken from its previous home for animal cruelty."

Frank teetered between tentative relief and fresh concern. "An abused animal? That could be dangerous…"

"She said they had a special program. The dog passed with flying colors."

Frank shook his head. "So did all of the Johnson dogs."

"What will Captain Errol say? You're right in the middle of this investigation."

Captain Errol, as it turned out, had no objection to Frank going to Florida to check on his daughter to make sure the dog wasn't one of the Johnson dogs. In fact, he said he was going as well.

"I don't believe she got one of our dogs," he said. "It's just too bizarre of a coincidence. But I'm going to come with you. We'll make sure she's okay and we'll find out where that Rottweiler went to. We'll get ahead of this one."

Frank choked up. He swallowed the hot lump in his throat, a few tears escaping his eyes. He was thankful Errol couldn't see him over the phone.

"Thank you, sir. I'm going to head over to the airport right now. I'll— we'll—catch the first flight out. I'll meet you there?"

"You'll get there before I will. Buy two tickets. The department will reimburse you for the trip to Louisiana too. I'll call you when I get to the airport and we'll meet up."

"Okay. See you soon."

CHAPTER NINETEEN

When they got off the plane, Errol picked up his voicemails. He turned his gaze toward Frank, the blood draining out of his face. He listened stoically to the rest of the message and pressed the 'end' button.

"Not Elsie," he told Frank immediately, getting that important detail out of the way.

Frank blew out his breath. "Okay," he said with more calm than he felt. "What happened?"

"A guide dog in Maine."

"Who did he kill? His owner?"

"She's not dead. But he tore off most of her face. She got too close to his kill, another dog that had strayed into his yard. She's in pretty serious shape. She will need extensive facial reconstruction. Lost a lot of blood. No one knew what had happened until hours later. The dog's already been destroyed. They'll check for rabies."

"None of the dogs have had rabies," Frank said. He shook his head. "At least rabies would make sense. This… this is just madness."

He swallowed back the fear and anxiety, tried to overcome the panic that made his heart race. "We have to get to Elsie. Right now."

"Okay. We're going."

————

There was no answer at Elsie's door.

Her car was there, parked in front, but no Elsie.

Frank took a quick trip around to the back yard, but it was empty. No Elsie. No dog.

Errol banged on the door.

Frank called Janice to tell her he was at Elsie's house and to see if by any chance Elsie had called her.

Janice's voice across the miles was tearful. "No, I haven't heard anything," she said. "Please… find my baby."

"I will, honey. I will."

Her tears galvanized him. Up until then, he had been relying on her strength, her sanity, to get him through this. Now, she needed him. He couldn't lean on her and her calm reason any longer. Now it was up to Frank to end the nightmare once and for all.

They knocked on the neighbors' doors, but no one could remember seeing Elsie over the last day or two. And none of them were close enough to have keys or to be able to tell him what kind of dog Elsie had adopted.

They looked at him with quizzical expressions and shrugged. What did it matter what kind of dog she had? It was big and black; that's all. She ran with him in the early morning and late evening, and he was never out in the yard barking. They didn't ever see him as anything other than a blur moving away through the darkness.

Frank cupped his hands to stare through the windows into the interior of Elsie's car. Why was her car still here? If she were at work, she would have the car with her, and the dog would be at home. She didn't run with the dog in the middle of the day. So where was she? And where was the dog? Frank straightened up and leaned his elbows on top of the sun-heated car, putting his face in his hands and trying to focus.

————

"Is there a problem, officer?"

Frank dropped his hands from his face, looking at the young woman approaching from the street.

"Daddy? What are you doing here?"

"Elsie! Oh, Elsie, you're okay!"

Frank hurried around the car and gave her a big hug, relieved beyond words, tears coursing down his face. Elsie hugged him back, then held him at arm's reach, brushing away tears with the back of her fingers.

"What is it, Daddy? What's wrong? Is Mom okay?"

"Yes, everybody is fine. Thank goodness *you're* okay."

"Well, why wouldn't I be?" she asked, puzzled. "I don't understand what you're doing here."

"Why didn't you call me back?"

"My phone is… broken. I have to get a new one. Did you leave me a message? I'm so sorry. I couldn't access the voicemail remotely; my PIN isn't working. Really, what's wrong? Is that all? I didn't return your call, so you flew out here?"

"It was more than one call," Frank said weakly.

For the first time, he looked down at the dog at her side. He saw with relief it was not a Rottweiler. All the anxiety flowed out of his body.

"I thought… I thought your dog had hurt you. I was worried something had happened to you."

"My dog? He wouldn't ever hurt me. I told you, he's very gentle."

"Dogs can be unpredictable," Frank explained. "And those dogs of the Johnsons… well… there's been some attacks. One of them came here and we couldn't trace it."

Elsie looked down at her dog, looking momentarily concerned, then she shook her head. "There's no way," she said. "He's very sweet."

"It was a Rottweiler," Frank said. "Not… whatever that is."

Elsie laughed. "A mutt," she said comfortably. "Well, would you and your friend like to come inside for a cup of coffee?"

Frank nodded. They all went inside. Frank and Errol sat on stools beside the counter while Elsie made the coffee.

"What are you doing home this time of day?" Frank asked. "I was worried when I saw the car here, but you didn't answer the door."

"I had to take Chief to the vet. It's just at a little strip mall a few blocks away."

"Is he okay?" Frank asked.

Elsie laughed. She dug into her purse and pulled out a cell phone. In several pieces. Turning it over in his hand, Frank could see teeth marks.

"He ate my cell phone. Some parts of it, anyway. We are taking x-rays every day until everything is out of his system, making sure it's all moving along properly…"

Frank looked at his daughter's wry expression and burst into laughter.

EPILOGUE

Frank sat in Elsie's living room, the TV playing sitcoms while she sent out some work emails. Chief had climbed onto the couch next to Frank and wouldn't be dissuaded from curling up in his favorite spot. His warm body was snuggled up against Frank's leg, and he was snoring and grumbling in his sleep. Frank's heart had raced when the big dog initially jumped up onto the couch, but it had now slowed, and he watched the dog's feet twitch in his sleep.

Frank's cellphone rang, and Chief's head went up, startled. Without thinking, Frank patted him on the head and scratched his ears. The dog put his head back down, making a noise almost like a purr as he settled back in.

It was Errol's name on the caller ID. He had checked into a local hotel for the night. "Captain?"

"They found the last dog," Errol reported.

"They found it?" Frank said. He exhaled. "That's all of them, then."

"That's all of them."

"Where is it?"

"Just a couple of counties over."

"And it didn't attack anyone? Everyone is okay?"

"Everyone is fine. It was harder to track because the kid who adopted it ended up selling it to someone else and never had his full name or address. But bylaw control ended up bringing it back in."

"Why? Did it get loose?"

"The dog was abused. Badly beaten. They were going to see if they could nurse it back to health, but… hearing the whole story, they've agreed to just put it down."

"So it's over. That's it now."

"That's all of them. Now you can rest easy."

Frank breathed in and out slowly.

Rest easy? Sleep without nightmares? He doubted it.

But one could dream.

Did you enjoy this book? Reviews and recommendations are vital to making a book successful.

Please leave a review at your favorite book store or review site and share it with your friends.

Don't miss the following bonus material:
Sign up for mailing list to get a free ebook
Read a sneak preview chapter
Other books by P.D. Workman
Learn more about the author

Sign up for my mailing list at pdworkman.com and get Gluten-Free Murder for free!

PREVIEW OF SHE WORE MOURNING

Zachary Goldman Mysteries #1

CHAPTER 1

ZACHARY GOLDMAN STARED DOWN the telephoto lens at the subjects before him. It was one of those days that left tourists gaping over the gorgeous scenery. Dark trees against crisp white snow, with the mountains as a backdrop. Like the picture on a Christmas card.

The thought made Zachary feel sick.

But he wasn't looking at the scenery. He was looking at the man and the woman in a passionate embrace. The pretty young woman's cheeks were flushed pink, more likely with her excitement than the cold, since she had barely stepped out of her car to greet the man. He had a swarthier complexion and a thin black beard, and was currently turned away from Zachary's camera.

Zachary wasn't much to look at himself. Average height, black hair cut too short, his own three-day growth of beard not hiding how pinched and pale his face was. He'd never considered himself a good catch.

He waited patiently for them to move, to look around at their surroundings so that he could get a good picture of their faces.

They thought they were alone; that no one could see them without being seen. They hadn't counted on the fact that Zachary had been surveilling them for a couple of weeks and had known where they would go. They gave him lots of warning so that he could park his car out of sight, camouflage himself in the trees, and settle in to wait for their appearance. He was no amateur; he'd been a private investigator since she had been choosing wedding dresses for her Barbie dolls.

He held down the shutter button to take a series of shots as they came up for air and looked around at the magnificent surroundings, smiling at each other, eyes shining.

All the while, he was trying to keep the negative thoughts at bay. Why had he fallen into private detection? It was one of the few ways he could make a living using his skill with a camera. He could have chosen another profession. He didn't need to spend his whole life following other people, taking pictures of their most private moments. What was the real point of his job? He destroyed lives, something he'd had his fill of long ago. When was the last time he'd brought a smile to a client's face? A real, genuine smile? He had wanted to make a difference in people's lives; to exonerate the innocent.

Zachary's phone started to buzz in his pocket. He lowered the camera and turned around, walking farther into the grove of trees. He had the pictures he needed. Anything else would be overkill.

He pulled out his phone and looked at it. Not recognizing the number, he swiped the screen to answer the call.

"Goldman Investigations."

"Uh… yes… Is this Mr. Goldman?" a voice inquired. Older, female, with a tentative quaver.

"Yes, this is Zachary," he confirmed, subtly nudging her away from the 'mister.'

"Mr. Goldman, my name is Molly Hildebrandt."

He hoped she wasn't calling her about her sixty-something-year-old husband and his renewed interest in sex. If it was another infidelity case, he was going to have to turn it down for his own sanity. He would even take a lost dog or wedding ring. As long as the ring wasn't on someone else's finger now.

"Mrs. Hildebrandt. How can Goldman Investigations help you?"

Of course, she had probably already guessed that Goldman Investigations consisted of only one employee. Most people seemed to sense that from the size of his advertisements. From the fact that he listed a post office box number instead of a business suite downtown or in one of the newer commercial areas. It wasn't really a secret.

"I don't know whether you have been following the news at all about Declan Bond, the little boy who drowned…?"

Zachary frowned. He trudged back toward his car.

"I'm familiar with the basics," he hedged. A four- or five-year-old boy whose round face and feathery dark hair had been pasted all over the news after a search for a missing child had ended tragically.

"They announced a few weeks ago that it was determined to be an accident."

Zachary ground his teeth. "Yes…?"

"Mr. Goldman, I was Declan's grandma." Her voice cracked. Zachary waited, listening to her sniffles and sobs as she tried to get herself under control. "I'm sorry. This has been very difficult for me. For everyone."

"Yes."

"Mr. Goldman, I don't believe that it was an accident. I'm looking for someone who would investigate the matter privately."

Zachary breathed out. A homicide investigation? Of a child? He'd told himself that he would take anything that wasn't infidelity, but if there was one thing that was more depressing than couples cheating on each other, it was the death of a child.

"I'm sure there are private investigators that would be more qualified for a homicide case than I am, Mrs. Hildebrandt. My schedule is pretty full right now."

Which, of course, was a lie. He had the usual infidelities, insurance investigations, liabilities, and odd requests. The dregs of the private investigation business. Nothing substantial like a homicide. It was a high-profile case. A lot of volunteers had shown up to help, expecting to find a child who had wandered out of his own yard, expecting to find him dirty and crying, not floating face down in a pond. A lot of people had mourned the death of a child they hadn't even known existed before his disappearance.

"I need your help, Mr. Goldman. Zachary. I can't afford a big name, but you've got good references. You've investigated deaths before. Can't you help me?"

He wondered who she had talked to. It wasn't like there were a lot of people who would give him a bad reference. He was competent and usually got the job done, but he wasn't a big name.

"I could meet with you," he finally conceded. "The first consultation is free. We'll see what kind of a case you have and whether I want to take it. I'm not making any promises at this point. Like I said, my schedule is pretty full already."

She gave a little half-sob. "Thank you. When are you able to come?"

———

After he had hung up, Zachary climbed into his car, putting his camera down on the floor in front of the passenger seat where it couldn't fall, and started the car. For a while, he sat there, staring out the front windshield at the magical, sparkling, Christmas-card scene. Every year, he told himself it would be better. He would get over it and be able to move on and to enjoy the holiday season like everyone else. Who cared about his crappy childhood experiences? People moved on.

And when he had married Bridget, he had thought he was going to achieve it. They would have a fairy-tale Christmas. They would have hot chocolate after skating at the public rink. They would wander down Main Street looking at the lights and the crèche in front of the church. They would open special, meaningful presents from each other.

But they'd fought over Christmas. Maybe it was Zachary's fault. Maybe he had sabotaged it with his gloom. The season brought with it so much baggage. There had been no skating rink. No hot chocolate, only hot tempers. No walks looking at the lights or the nativity. They had practically thrown their gifts at each other, flouncing off to their respective corners to lick their wounds and pout away the holiday.

He'd still cherished the thought that perhaps the next year there would be a baby. What could be more perfect than Christmas with a baby? It would unite them. Make them a real family. Just like Zachary had longed for since he'd lost his own family. He and Bridget and a baby. Maybe even twins. Their own little family in their own little happy bubble.

But despite a positive pregnancy test, things had gone horribly wrong.

Zachary stared at the bright white scenery and blinked hard, trying to shake off the shadows of the past. The past was past. Over and done. This year he was back to baching it for Christmas. Just him and a beer and *It's a Wonderful Life* on TV.

He put the car in reverse and didn't look into the rear-view mirror as he backed up, even knowing about the precipice behind him. He'd deliberately parked where he'd have to back up toward the cliff when he was done. There was a guardrail, but if he backed up too quickly, the car would go right through it, and who could say whether it had been accidental or deliberate? He had been cold-stone sober and had been out on a job. Mrs. Hildebrandt could testify that he had been calm and sober during their call. It would be ruled an accident.

But his bumper didn't even touch the guardrail before he shifted into drive and pulled forward onto the road.

He'd meet with the grandmother. Then, assuming he did not take the case, there would always be another opportunity.

Life was full of opportunities.

CHAPTER 2

Molly Hildebrandt was much as Zachary expected her to be. A woman in her sixties who looked ten or twenty years older with the stress of the high-profile death of her grandchild. Gray, curling hair. Pale, wrinkled skin. She wasn't hunched over, though. She sat up straight and tall as if she'd gone to a finishing school where she'd been forced to walk and sit with an encyclopedia on her head. Did they still do that? Had they ever done it?

"Mr. Goldman, thank you for seeing me so quickly," she greeted formally, holding her hand out for him to shake when he arrived at her door.

"Please, call me Zachary, ma'am. I'm not really comfortable with Mr. Goldman."

Telling her that he wasn't comfortable with it meant that she would be a bad hostess if she continued to address him that way, instead of her seeing it as a way of showing him respect. He hadn't done anything to deserve respect and was much happier if she would talk to him like the gardener or her next-door neighbor.

Not that there was any gardener. Molly lived in a small apartment in an old, dark brick building that was sturdy enough, but had been around longer than Zachary had been alive. The interior, when she invited him in, was bright and cozy. She had made coffee, and he breathed in the aroma in the air appreciatively. It wasn't hot chocolate after skating, but he could use a cup or two of coffee to warm him up after his surveillance. Standing around in the snow for a couple of hours had chilled him, even though he'd dressed for the weather.

Molly escorted him to the tiny living room.

"And you must call me Molly," she insisted.

She eyed the big camera case as he put it down. Zachary gave a grimace.

"Sorry. I didn't come to take your picture; I just don't like to leave expensive equipment in the car."

"Oh," she nodded politely. She didn't ask him who he had been taking pictures of. That wouldn't be gracious. She would have to imagine instead, and she would probably be correct in her guess.

They fussed for a few minutes with their coffees. Zachary wrapped his fingers around his mug, waiting for the coffee to cool and his fingers to warm. It felt good. Comforting. He waited for Molly to begin her story.

"You probably think that I'm just being a fussy old lady," she said. "Imagining something sinister when it was just an accident."

"Not at all. Why don't you tell me why you don't think it was an accident?"

"I'm not *sure* at all," she clarified. "Maybe they're right. Maybe it was an accident. It isn't that I doubt their findings..." she trailed off. "Not really. I know they had to do an autopsy and all that. We waited for months for them to come back with the manner of death. I thought that once they ruled, everyone would feel better."

"But you still have doubts?"

"I'm worried for my daughter."

Zachary blinked at her and waited for more.

"She's not well. I had hoped that once they released the body... and after the memorial... and after the manner of death was announced... each milestone, I thought, it would get better. It would be easier for her, but..." Molly shook her head. "She's getting worse and worse. Time isn't helping."

"Your daughter was Declan's mother."

"Yes. Of course."

"What's her name?"

"Isabella Hildebrandt," Molly said, her brows drawn down like he should have known that. "You know. *The Happy Artist.*"

Zachary had heard of *The Happy Artist.* She was on TV and was popular among the locals. Zachary didn't know whether she was syndicated nationally or just on one of the local stations. She had a painting instruction show every Sunday morning, and people awaited her next show like a popular soap. Most of the people Zachary knew who watched the show didn't paint and never intended to take it up. She was an institution.

"Oh, yes," Zachary agreed. "Of course, I know *The Happy Artist.* I didn't put the names together."

"When it was in the news, they said who she was. They said it was *The Happy Artist*'s child."

"Sure. Of course," Zachary agreed. He rubbed the dark stubble along his jaw. He should have gone home to shave and clean up before meeting with Molly. He looked like he'd been on a three-day stakeout. He *had* been on a three-day stakeout. "I'm sorry. I didn't follow the story very closely. That's good for you; it means I don't have a lot of preconceived ideas about the case."

She looked at him for a minute, frowning. Reconsidering whether she really wanted to hire him? That wouldn't hurt his feelings.

"You were going to tell me about your daughter?" Zachary prompted. "I can understand how devastated she must be by her son's death."

"No. I don't think you can," Molly said flatly.

Zachary was taken aback. He shrugged and nodded, and waited for her to go on.

"Isabella has a history of… mental health issues. She was the one supervising Declan when he disappeared, and the guilt has been overwhelming for her."

That made perfect sense. Zachary sipped at his coffee, which had cooled enough not to scald him.

Molly went on. "I think… as horrible as it may sound… that it would be a relief for her if it turned out that Declan was taken from the yard, instead of just having wandered away."

"That may be, but how likely is that? Surely the police must have considered the possibility, and I can't manufacture evidence for your daughter, even if it would ease her mind."

"No… I realize that. I'm not expecting you to do anything dishonest. Just to investigate it. Read over the police reports. Interview witnesses again. Just see… if there's any possibility that there was… foul play. A third-party interfering, even if it was nothing malicious."

"I assume you know most of the details surrounding the case."

"Yes, of course."

"How likely do you think it is that the police missed something? Did they seem sloppy or like they didn't care? Did you think there were signs of foul play that they brushed off?"

"No." Molly gave a little shrug. "They seemed perfectly competent."

Zachary was silent. It wouldn't be difficult to read over the police reports and talk to the family. Was there any point?

"The only thing is…" Molly trailed off.

As impatient as Zachary was to get out of there, he knew it was no good pushing Molly to give it up any faster. She already knew she sounded crazy for asking him to reinvestigate a case where he wasn't going to be able to turn up anything new. For no reason, other than that it might help her daughter to come to terms with the child's death. He looked around the room. There were no pictures of Molly's husband, even old ones. There was no sign she had raised Isabella or any other children there. There were several pictures of a couple with a little child. Declan and Isabella and whatever the father's name was. There was one picture of Declan himself, occupying its own space, a little memorial to her lost grandson. There were no pictures of anyone else, so Zachary could only assume Isabella was an only child and Declan the only grandchild.

"Declan was afraid of water."

Zachary turned his eyes back to her. He considered. It wasn't totally inconceivable that a child afraid of the water would drown. He wouldn't know how to swim. If he fell in, he would panic, flail, and swallow water, rather than staying calm enough to float. Molly wiped at a tear.

"How afraid of the water was he?" Zachary asked.

"He wouldn't go near the water. He was terrified. He wouldn't have gone to the pond by himself."

"How tall was he?"

Molly gave a little shrug. "He was almost five years old. Three feet?"

"How steep were the banks of the pond and what was the terrain and foliage like?" He knew he would have to look at it for himself.

"I don't know what you want to know… there wasn't any shore to speak of. Just the pond. There were bulrushes. Cattails. Some trees. The ground is… uneven, but not hilly."

Zachary tried to visualize it. A child wouldn't be able to see the pond as far away as an adult would because of his short stature. If his view were further screened by the plant life, the banks steep and crumbly, he might not be able to see it until he was right on top of it. Or in it.

"It's not a lot to go on," he said. "The fact that he was afraid of water."

"I know." Molly used both hands to wipe her eyes. "I know that." She looked around the apartment, swallowing hard to get control of her emotions. "I just want the best for my baby. A parent always wants what's best. Growing up… I wasn't able to give her that. She didn't have an easy life. I wonder if…" She didn't have to finish the sentence this time. Zachary already knew what she was going to say. She wondered if that rough upbringing had caused Isabella's mental fragility. Whether things would have turned out differently if she'd been able to provide a stable environment. Molly sniffled. "Do you have children, Mr.—Zachary?"

Zachary felt that familiar pain in his chest. Like she'd plunged a knife into it. He cleared his throat and shook his head. "No. My marriage just recently ended. We didn't have any children."

"Oh." Her eyes searched his for the truth. Zachary looked away. "I'm sorry. I guess we all have our losses."

Although hers, the death of her grandson, was clearly more permanent than any relationship issues Zachary might have.

———

In the end, he agreed to do the preliminaries. Get the police reports. Walk the area around the house and pond. Talk to the parents. He gave her his lowest hourly fee. She clearly couldn't afford more. He wasn't even sure she'd be able to pay on receipt of his invoice. He might have to allow her a payment plan, something he normally didn't do, but something about the frail woman had gotten to him.

He put in an appearance at the police station, requesting a copy of the information available to the public, and handing over Molly Hildebrandt's request that he be provided as much information as possible for an independent evaluation.

"You got a new case?" Bowman grunted as he tapped through a few computer screens, getting a feel for how many files there were on the Declan Bond accident investigation file and how much of it he would be able to provide to Zachary.

"Yes," Zachary agreed. Obviously. He didn't encourage small talk; he really didn't want Bowman to start asking personal questions. They weren't friends, but they were friendly. Bowman had helped Zachary track down missing documents before. He knew the right people to ask for permission and the best way to ask.

Bowman dug into his pocket and pulled out a pack of gum. He unwrapped a piece and popped it into his mouth, then offered one to Zachary as an afterthought.

"No, I'm good."

Bowman chewed vigorously as he studied each screen. He was a middle-aged man, with a middle-age spread, his belly sagging over his belt. His hairline had started receding, and occasionally he put on a pair of glasses for a moment and then took them off again, jamming them into his breast pocket.

"How's Bridget?" he asked.

Zachary swallowed. He took a deep breath and steeled himself for the conversation. Bowman looked away from his screen and at Zachary's face, eyebrows up.

"She's good. In remission."

"Good to hear." Bowman looked back at his computer again. "Good to hear. It's been a tough time for the two of you." His eyes flicked back to Zachary, and he backtracked. "I mean it's been tough for her. And for you."

"Yeah," Zachary agreed. He waved away any further fumbling explanation from Bowman. "So, what have we got? On the Bond case?"

"Right!" Bowman looked back at his screen. "I've got press releases and public statements for you. medical examiner's report. The cop in charge of the file was Eugene. He likes red."

Zachary blinked at Bowman, more baffled than usual by his abbreviated language. "What?"

"Eugene Taft. I know, it's a preposterous name, but he's never had a nickname that stuck. Eugene Taft."

"And he likes red."

"Wine," Bowman said as if Zachary was dense. "He likes red wine. You know, if you want to help things along, have a better chance of getting a look at the rest of that file, the officers' notes and all the background and interviews. If you have to apply some leverage."

"And for Eugene Taft, it's red wine."

"Has to be red," Bowman confirmed.

"Okay." Zachary looked at his watch. "Can you start that stuff printing for me? Is there anyone downstairs?" He knew he would have to run down to the basement to order a copy of the medical examiner's report. Just one of those bureaucratic things.

"Sure. Kenzie should be down there still."

Zachary paused. "Kenzie. Not Bradley?"

"Kenzie," Bowman confirmed. "She's new."

"How new?"

"I don't know." Bowman gave a heavy shrug. "How long since you were down there last? Less than that."

Zachary snorted and went down the hall to the elevator.

As he waited for it, Joshua Campbell, an officer he'd worked with on an insurance fraud case several months previous, approached and hit the up button. He did a double-take, looking at Zachary.

"Zach Goldman! How are you, man? Haven't seen you around here lately."

"Good." Zachary shook hands with him. Joshua's hands were hard and rough like he'd grown up working on a farm instead of in the city. Zachary wondered what he did in his spare time that left them so rough and scarred. He wasn't boxing after work; Zachary would have been able to tell that by his knuckles. "Hey, how's Bridget doing? Did everything turn out okay…?" He trailed off and shifted uncomfortably.

"Yeah, great. She's in remission."

"Oh, good. That's great, Zach. Good to hear."

Zachary nodded politely. His elevator arrived with a ding and a flashing down indicator. Zachary sketched a quick goodbye to Joshua and jumped on. He was starting to regret agreeing to look into the Bond case.

The girl at the desk had dark, curly hair, red-lipsticked lips, and a tight, slim form. She was working through some forms, those red lips pursed in concentration, and she didn't look up at him.

"Hang on," she said. "Just let me finish this part up, before I lose my train of thought."

Zachary stood there as patiently as possible, which wasn't too hard with a pretty girl to look at. She finally filled in the last space and looked up at him. She raised an eyebrow.

"You must be Kenzie," Zachary said.

"I don't know if I must be, but I am. Kenzie Kirsch. And you are?"

"Zachary Goldman. From Goldman Investigations."

"A private investigator?"

"Yes."

He didn't usually introduce himself that way because it gave people funny ideas about the kind of life he lived and how he spent his time. Most people did not think about mounds of paperwork or painstaking accident scene reconstructions when they thought about private investigation. They thought about Dick Tracy and Phillip Marlowe and all the old hardboiled detectives. When really most of a private investigator's life was mind-numbingly boring, and he didn't need to carry a gun.

"And what can I do for you today, Mr. Private Investigator?"

"Zachary."

"Zachary," she repeated, losing the teasing tone and giving him a warm smile. "What can I do for you?"

"I need to order a copy of a medical examiner's report. Declan Bond."

"Bond. That's the boy? The drowning victim?"

"That's the one."

She looked at him, shaking her head slightly. "Why do you need that one? It's closed. A determination was made that it was an accident."

"I know. The family would like someone else to look at it. Just to set their minds at ease."

"You're not going to find anything. It's an open-and-shut case."

"That's fine. They just want someone to take a look. It's not a reflection on the medical examiner. You know how families are. They need to be able to move on. They're not quite ready to let it go yet. One last attempt to understand…"

Kenzie gave a little shrug. "Okay, then… there's a form…" She bent over and searched through a drawer full of files to find the right one. Zachary had filled them out before. Usually, he could manage to do an end-run and Bradley would just pull the file for him. Officially, he was supposed to fill one out. He didn't want to end up in hot water with the new administrator, so he leaned on the counter and filled the form out carefully.

She went on with her own forms and filing, not trying to fill the silence with small talk. Which Zachary thought was nice. When he was finished, he put the pen back in its holder and handed the form to Kenzie. To the side of the work she was doing. Not right in front of her face. She again ignored him while she finished the section she was on, then picked it up to look it over.

"You have nice printing," she observed, her voice going up slightly. She laughed at herself. "No reason why you shouldn't," she said quickly. "It's just that the majority of the forms that get submitted here are… well, to say they were chicken scratch would be insulting to chickens."

Zachary chuckled. "That's the difference between a cop and a private investigator."

"Neat handwriting?"

"Yeah. Cops have to fill out so many forms, they don't care. You can just call them if you need something clarified. Me… I know if I don't fill it out right, it's just going to go in the circular file." He nodded in the direction of the garbage can.

"I wouldn't throw it out," she protested.

"If you couldn't read it? What else would you do?"

"I would at least try to call you."

Zachary indicated the form. "That's why I printed my phone number so neatly."

Kenzie smiled and nodded. "It's very clear," she approved.

"You'll call me?"

"I'll let you know when it's ready to be picked up."

Zachary hovered there for an extra few seconds. He was enjoying the give-and-take of his conversation with her but didn't want her to accuse him of being creepy. He wasn't the type who asked a girl out the first time he saw her.

He gave her another smile and walked away from the desk. Maybe next time.

———

She Wore Mourning, book #1 of the *Zachary Goldman Mysteries* series is available now at pdworkman.com

www.ingramcontent.com/pod-product-compliance
Lightning Source LLC
Chambersburg PA
CBHW061308210726
48293CB00003B/1173